Chapter 132
Fruits Basket

IT SEEMED LIKE HE WAS ALWAYS JUST FINE BEING ON HIS OWN.
THAT IRRITATED ME, ODDLY ENOUGH.
SHIGURE...
DO YOU LOVE ME?

I WANTED TO SEE IF I COULD MAKE HIM PAY ATTENTION TO ME.

IS EVERYONE HERE?
AYA-NII... WENT OFF SOME-WHERE.
MM...
GREAT...
YUKI...
WHAT HAPPENED TO SHIGURE?
HUH?
HE'S NOT HERE?
HE LEFT THE HOUSE EARLY THIS MORNING...
...THAT SO?
LOOKS LIKE THE KIDS ARE MORE DEPENDABLE THAN THE ADULTS...
WHA...!!?

THANK
I'M SORRY! I'M SORRY! I'M SORRY FOR NOT BEING A DECENT ADULT!!
EEEEEEEK!
I'M SORRRRRRRY!!
...
WHY DON'T YOU QUIT DRESSING LIKE A WOMAN ALREADY ...?
RITSU HASN'T CHANGED, HUH...?
SO WE ALL SHOWED UP...
...LIKE WE WERE TOLD...
...BUT AKITO...
...KNOWS... WHAT HAPPENED WITH US, RIGHT?
I'M...
...KINDA WORRIED ...

...THINGS MIGHT BE A BIT TENSE...
...HEY.
......
HEY.
NOOO, NOT "HEY" !!!
GABAA (GLOMP)
WHOA!
WH-WHAT THE...!? WHAT'S WRONG!!?
AAAH! I CAN'T TAKE IT ANYMORE! I CAN'T TAKE IT! I DON'T UNDERSTAND, DAMMIT!
I CAN'T TAKE ANY OF THIS ANY-MORE!!

BASHA (FLASH)
...CHEATING ALREADY...?
THAT MAKES YOU...
...THE LOWEST OF THE LOW!
WHA...!? THAT'S NOT WHAT...!
YOU'RE THE WORST...
HE'S THE WORST! ♪
WAS THAT A TRAP!? ARE YOU TWO OUT TO GET ME!?

...IT'LL BE OKAY.
TENSE, HUH?
...I ACTUALLY DON'T THINK THAT'S LIKELY.
...WELL, I WAS A LITTLE WORRIED BEFORE...
...THAT IF THE CURSE BROKE...
...WE'D FEEL AWKWARD AROUND EACH OTHER, BUT...
NO WORRIES THERE... I'LL ALWAYS LOVE YOU......
AH. YEAH. THANKS. RIN'S WATCHING, BY THE WAY.
SHE'S WATCHING WITH LASER EYES!!

しゃばだばぁ…
SHABADABAAAN (FWISH)
AS WILL I, YUKI...
I'LL ALWAYS BE WATCHING OVER YOU CLOSELY...
...YOU WEREN'T EVEN HERE 'TIL JUST NOW, SO THAT DOESN'T REALLY CARRY ANY WEIGHT.
WORRY NOT, MY BROTHER! I COULD NEVER FEEL AWKWARD AROUND YOU. AS A WISE MAN ONCE SAID...
..."IF EVERYONE CROSSES AT THE RED LIGHT TOGETHER, THERE'S NOTHING TO FEAR!"
THAT'S NOT A REAL PROVERB...
WEL-COME BACK...
IF ALL OF US ARE RELEASED FROM THE CURSE, THEN ALL OF US ARE EXHILARATED!
BUT ALSO...
...THE FACT OF THE MATTER IS—NO MATTER WHAT HAPPENS, MY CHARISMATIC ELEGANCE SHALL NEVER FADE, SO FEEL FREE TO WORSHIP AT MY ALTAR!
THAT'S WHAT YOU REALLY WANTED TO SAY, HUH?
AYA-NIISAN...!! HE'S SO COOL...!!

WHAT THE HELL...?
AKITO'S STILL NOT OUT YET...?
YOU SOUND IMPATIENT, KYONKICHI, BUT WERE YOU NOT JUST WANDERING AROUND SOME-WHERE?
BISHI (POINT)
HUH!? YEAH, BUT...
WAS DOING THE SAME THING JUST BEFORE
...THIS IS ONLY MY... SECOND TIME COMIN' TO THE MAIN HOUSE...?
OR THIRD TIME?
...SO I WAS CURIOUS ......
AH!
I SEE, I SEE!
A PEASANT LIKE YOU MUST BE OVERWHELMED BY THIS MANSION'S VASTNESS AND OPULENCE, BUT DON'T BE TIMID, KYONKICHI! ROAM AROUND TO YOUR HEART'S CONTENT!!
AHAHAHAHA
ON YOUR HIGH HORSE AGAIN, HUH? WHEN YOU AIN'T EVEN THE OWNER OF THIS PLACE...
HEY...
HAHAHAHAHAHAHAHA
WHY DON'T YOU TAKE HOME A PAIR OF SLIPPERS AS A SOUVENIR?
THAT'D MAKE ME A THIEF...
MY BROTHER IS IMPRESSIVE IN HIS OWN WAY... INSTEAD OF TIPTOEING AROUND KYO, THE FORMER CAT...
...HE'S AS RUDE AS EVER...? WOW......

EVERY-ONE...
IF I COULD PLEASE HAVE YOUR ATTEN-TION...
AKITO-SAN IS READY TO SEE YOU...

......
HATORI...
WHERE IS SHIGURE?
...
I DON'T KNOW.
...... AH—
AKITO-SAN... COULD IT BE!?
WE SHARE THE SAME...
...HOBBY...?
NO...
THIS IS...

A PRESENT, FROM ME TO YOU.
YOU COULD CALL IT A "PARTING GIFT."

....
GA (WHAP)
I HATE YOU...!!
OW...
I HATE YOU...
I DESPISE YOU!
I KNEW THIS WOULD HAPPEN!
I ALWAYS KNEW...
OUCH!
...YOU'D BE THE FIRST TO ABANDON ME!!
I HATE YOU...
I HATE YOU!
I DESPISE YOU!!
WHO EXACTLY ...

...DO YOU THINK I'M "ABANDONING," HERE?
......
...B—
BUT YOU SAID "PARTING GIFT"—
YOU'RE FINALLY SAYING "GOODBYE" TO THE PERSON YOUR FATHER WANTED YOU TO BE...
...AND CHANGING INTO A "NEW YOU," RIGHT?
HENCE A "PARTING GIFT."
A PRESENT.
...CON-GRATULA-TIONS.
I WELCOME...
...THE NEW YOU.

I LOOK FORWARD TO SEEING...
...HOW YOU'RE GOING TO LIVE YOUR LIFE FROM HERE ON OUT.
...
JUST AS ALL OF YOU...
...HAVE FINALLY...
...BEEN ABLE TO RETURN... TO YOUR NATURAL FORMS...
...I TOO...
...
...AM RETURNING TO MY...
...TRUE FORM.
ALL OF YOU ARE FREE.
AND THIS...
...MAY COME TOO LATE...
...BUT FOR EVERYTHING...

...EVERY-THING...
...UP TO NOW...
I'M ......
AFTER ALL THE TERRIBLE THINGS...
......
...YOU'VE DONE TO THEM...
......
AFTER ALL THE SUFFERING YOU'VE CAUSED...

...I'M CURIOUS ABOUT...
...HOW YOU'RE GOING TO ATONE FOR EVERYTHING GOING FORWARD.
...!
SHUT UP! YOU'RE ALWAYS—
PASHI (WHAP)
YOU CARE ABOUT WHAT I THINK?
I'M HONORED.
I DO NOT!!
I......
......!
...
IT... IT'S NOT THAT.
SHIGURE...
MORE THAN ANYONE...
YOU'VE ALWAYS...
...SCARED ME THE MOST...

IT ALWAYS FELT LIKE...
...YOU WERE THE FURTHEST AWAY FROM ME.
...AND ACT LIKE I DIDN'T CARE...
OTHERWISE, IT FELT LIKE I'D EXPLODE......
YOU WERE THE ONE I COULDN'T PIN DOWN. YOU WERE NEVER AFRAID OF ME LIKE THE OTHERS.
I HAD TO STAY CALM...
...EVEN WHEN I THOUGHT I HAD YOU...
EVEN THOUGH WE ALL HAD A "BOND"...
...YOU WERE THE MOST DISTANT OF ALL, SHIGURE...
...YOU FLUTTERED AWAY...
...TO SOME-ONE ELSE'S LAP, DIDN'T YOU?

...
TRAITOR.
TH...
B—
BUT I DID THAT BECAUSE...
SHIGURE, YOU—
I'VE ALWAYS BEEN A CUNNING, IMMATURE GUY.
ONCE I GET MY HANDS ON SOMETHING, I NEVER WANT TO GIVE IT BACK...
...OR LET ANYONE ELSE TOUCH IT.
THAT'S WHY I CAN'T STAND BEING HURT...
...OR GETTING THE SHORT END OF THE STICK.

......
GATA (RATTLE)
YEAH... IF YOU'RE GOING TO REJECT ME...
...NOW'S THE TIME.
THANKS TO YOU, I BELIEVE I'VE LEARNED HOW TO BE GENEROUS, TO AN EXTENT...
...SO I'LL GIVE YOU TIME TO RUN AWAY IF THAT'S WHAT YOU REALLY WANT.
...WA—
BUT YOU SHOULD KNOW...
...IF YOU DO CHOOSE ...
...TO COME TO ME ONCE MORE...

...WELL, WE'LL BOTH KNOW WHAT THAT MEANS, RIGHT?
......YOU'RE CRUEL.
THAT'S NOT FAIR.
AS IF YOU WERE NEVER...
...AT FAULT FOR ANY OF THIS.
YOU REALLY ARE A CHILD.
AND YET...
...YOU HAD THAT SAME LOOK IN YOUR EYES...
...AS IF TO SAY, "I'LL BE FINE ON MY OWN."
IT'S BEYOND IRRITAT-ING.
I WANT TO MAKE YOU PAY ATTENTION TO ME.
I WANT TO...

...DRINK UP EVERY PART OF YOU.
DOWN TO YOUR CELLS...
DOWN TO THE MARROW OF YOUR BONES...
I WANT TO LEAVE MY MARK...
...DEEP, DEEP INSIDE YOU.
I WANT TO DRINK YOU UP, FILL YOU WITH MY SCENT...
...UNTIL YOU CAN'T BREATHE.

THIS FEELING...
THIS DESIRE...
IS IT COMING FROM WITHIN ME, AS A WOMAN?
...EVERYONE...
...WAS SURPRISED.
THEY SEEMED TO HAVE...
...MIXED FEELINGS.
I TRIED TO APOLOGIZE...
...BUT I WASN'T ABLE TO.
WHEN I TRIED FORMING THE WORDS...
...IT WAS AS IF I WERE SAYING...
..."SO LET THIS BE THE END OF IT."

I...
I'M GOING TO...
...CON-TINUE...
...LIVING HERE, I THINK.
I BELIEVE THERE ARE THINGS...
...I STILL NEED TO DO.
IN ORDER...
...TO PROTECT ...
...THEIR TRUE FREEDOM ...
AFTER ALL...
...I AM STILL...
...THE HEAD OF THE FAMILY...

IN OTHER WORDS ...
...YOU WANT ME TO STICK AROUND WITH YOU FOR THAT KIND OF LIFE?
...
ARE YOU ANGRY?
...
A LITTLE.
I MEAN...
...I'VE BEEN WAITING...
...FOR SO, SO LONG...
...FOR YOU TO COME BACK TO ME.
... THAT'S WHY...
...I NEED...
...TO ALSO TALK TO...
...REN.
LEAVE!

YOU KEPT ME WAITING, DIDN'T YOU?
YOU'RE BEAUTI-FUL.
...THAT SUITS YOU.
I GET CHILLS...
...WHEN YOU...

...TURN TO LOOK AT ME.
...I LOVE YOU.
I LOVE YOU ......
I LOVE YOU SO MUCH.

I'LL LOVE YOU FOREVER, AS LONG AS YOU WANT ME TOO.

Chapter 133

OH!
THERE'S KYO-KUN!
SHOULD I CALL OUT TO HIM!?
THINK HE'S HEADING HOME!?
HE'S WAITING FOR HIS GIRLFRIEND, ISN'T HE?
SAY WHAT!?
G-GIRL-FRIEND...
WHAT DO YOU MEAN, GIRL-FRIEND!?
WHO IS SHE!?
HUH?
HONDA-SAN. SHE'S IN MY CLASS.
TOHRU HONDA-SAN.

HONDA-SAN WAS HOSPITALIZED FOR A WHILE...
...AND MISSED FINALS...
THREE MINUTES LEFT!
...SO SHE'S RETAKING THEM BY HERSELF TODAY.
HE'S GOTTA BE WAITING FOR HER TO FINISH, RIGHT?
LOOK, HE JUST WENT BACK IN.
I THINK SOMETIME AFTER HONDA-SAN GOT OUT OF THE HOSPITAL?
THOSE TWO WERE JOINED AT THE HIP MORE THAN BEFORE, SO WHEN OUR CLASSMATES TEASED THEM...
WHAT HAVE WE HERE?
ARE YOU TWO FINALLY GOING OUT?
I-I DON'T BELIEVE IT...
WHEN DID THIS HAPPEN ...?
YEAH.
?
WHAT ABOUT IT?

WHOAAA!
HE JUST CAME RIGHT OUT AND SAID IT!! HE SAID IT LIKE IT'S NO BIG DEAL!!
THE KID WHO WAS SO SCARED OF GIRLS THE FIRST DAY HE TRANSFERRED THAT HE JUMPED OUT A WINDOW! AND NOW HE'S "MR. SMOOTH"!!
THE BOY... THE BOY'S BECOME A MAN!!!
SHADDAP.
CELEBRATE...
WE HAVE TO CELEBRATE!
WHAT'S UP?
RED RICE...
WE'VE GOTTA HAVE RED RICE!
WHAT'S GOING ON?
WHY ARE WE CHEERING?
NO, WE DON'T.
...UH.
OF COURSE THEY'D MAKE A BIG THING OF IT...
......
WAAAAH...
I'M SHOCKED!
THIS IS AWFUL...
MY DREAMS ARE SMASHED NOW THAT HE BELONGS TO SOMEBODY ELSE...
MY DEEPEST SYMPA-THIES.

TIIIME'S UP!
GOOD WORK.
Y......
YES
THANK YOU... VERY MUCH...
HOW WAS IT?
KASA (RUSTLE)
W...
WELL... I TRIED... WITH ALL MY MIGHT...
DOESN'T SEEM LIKE SHE HAD A LOT OF MIGHT......
WELL.
NOW GO ENJOY THE REST OF YOUR LAST HIGH SCHOOL SUMMER VACATION.
AH...
YES!
...OH.
THAT'S RIGHT, HONDA.
THANK
YOU

HAS SOMETHING HAPPENED RECENTLY...
...AT THE SOHMA HOUSE...?
...YESTER-DAY...
...THOSE TWO...
...LOOKED LIKE THEY WERE HAVING A GOOD TIME...
HUH...?
WHAT DO YOU MEAN...
HUH!? AH! WHA...!?
...BY "SOME-THING" !?
HMM...
"HAVING A GOOD TIME"...?
DO YOU MEAN KYO-KUN AND YUKI-KUN?
HUH!?
THOSE TWO!!
Y-YEAH! THAT'S WHO I MEAN!!
SHUTA (WHOOSH)
W-W-WELL, WHATEVER! IT DOESN'T MATTER!!
ANYWAY, BE CAREFUL GOING HOME!!
AH...
GARA (RATTLE)
GARA

...?
"HAS SOMETHING HAPPENED?"
QUITE A BIT, ACTUALLY.
FOR INSTANCE, AKITO-SAN REVEALING HERSELF AS A WOMAN...
...TO EVERYONE.
I WAS SPEECHLESS...
...YOU KNOW?
HONESTLY, I'M MORE SURPRISED THAT YOU COULD KEEP A SECRET LIKE THAT.
THAT TOO...
I-I'M SORRY. UM...
I KNEW, BUT DIDN'T KNOW IF I SHOULD BRING IT UP...
...

WAS IT...
...A SHOCK TO YOU TOO?
A "SHOCK" ...?
...I GUESS.
WELL, ANYWAY...
...I WAS DUMBSTRUCK.
....
...SORRY, I CAN'T REALLY EXPLAIN IT WELL...
...BE-CAUSE SO MUCH...
...HAS HAPPENED ......
...AS FOR ME...
BUT...
...I DIDN'T KNOW IT AT THE TIME, BUT I STILL CAN'T BELIEVE I WAS SO VIOLENT...
...TO A GIRL.

...I WAS ALSO A LITTLE RELIEVED.
HUH?
"RELIEVED" ...? HOW SO?
...HOW CAN I PUT IT?
THE LAST THING I WANTED...
...WAS YET ANOTHER GUY INTERESTED IN YOU.
PFFT!
...HEY!
HEH HEH HEH
I'M NOT LAUGHING ...
HEH HEH
I'M NOT LAUGHING AT ALL...
YOU OBVIOUSLY ARE LAUGHIN'...
YOU ARE SO SMALL-MINDED...
LATELY, I'VE NOTICED...
...THAT THE MOOD BETWEEN THEM...
HEH HEH HEH.
...HAS BECOME SOMEWHAT GENTLER THAN BEFORE.

WHEN I TRIED ASKING HIM...
...WHY THAT WAS...
HE BEAT THE CRAP OUTTA ME.
...HA!
JUST KIDDIN'.
HUH!!?
HE HIT ME SO HARD, THE BIGGEST SCREW IN MY HEAD CAME LOOSE AND WENT FLYING.
WHA ...!?
I TELL YA, THAT GUY'S BAD NEWS. DON'T EVER TALK TO HIM AGAIN.
WHAT !!?

KYO-KUN...
...SMILES A LOT MORE NOW, THAT'S FOR SURE.
AND I'VE COME TO REALIZE...
!
...THAT THIS IS HIS TRUE SELF.
KYO-KUN...!
TOTE (TROT) TE TE TE TE
???
KYO...
KYO-KU—

KYO-KUN...!
YOU WAITED FOR ME...!?
YEAH... WELL.
GOOD JOB ON THE TEST.
ALL RIGHT, ALL RIGHT...
WHAT ARE YOU, A PUPPY?
GYUUU (TUG)
ぎう
THANK YOU... YOU WEREN'T TOO BORED WAITING, WERE YOU!?
NAH, IT WAS FINE.
I WAS PLAYIN' BASKETBALL WITH SOME OF OUR CLASSMATES FIRST.
THOSE GUYS SURE HAVE A LOT OF ENERGY, CONSIDERIN' HOW HOT IT IS!
AH-HA-HA!
I CAN TELL THAT EVERYONE AROUND US...
...IS DRAWN TO KYO-KUN EVEN MORE, NOW THAT HE'S LIKE THIS.
SWEAR
IT'S A MIRACLE.
...COMPARED TO THE GUYS WHO'RE GOIN' TO COLLEGE...
...THE ONES WHO PLAN ON GETTIN' A JOB STRAIGHT AWAY ARE STILL ALL HAPPY-GO-LUCKY, HUH?
NOT MY PROBLEM THOUGH...

THAT'S... RIGHT...
ME TOO......
I HAVE TO... GET SERIOUS ABOUT...JOB HUNTING...
TOTALLY FORGOT ABOUT IT
......
HEY.
DO YOU...
...WANNA ...?
Y... YES?
......
NAH.
NEVER MIND. I'LL TALK TO YOU ABOUT IT...LATER.
MORE IMPORTANTLY...
...LOOKIN' FOR A JOB IS ALL WELL AND GOOD...
?
...BUT IT'S SUMMER VACATION!
SO LET'S...
...JUST THE TWO OF US...

...GO PLACES. A LOT OF PLACES.
...
...R...
RIGHT!!
A LOT OF PLACES... FOR SURE!!
COOL, SOUNDS LIKE A PLAN.
THAT'S A PROMISE.
OH!
UO-CHAN AND HANA-CHAN...
...SAID THEY REALLY WANT TO GO WITH US THE FIRST TIME WE GO OUT...!
AH...
...WELL.
CAN'T HELP THAT, I GUESS.
THOSE TWO ARE LIKE YOUR SURROGATE PARENTS...

IT'S A MIRACLE...
...THAT I CAN BE WITH KYO-KUN...
...LIKE THIS.
I WANT TO...
...MAKE THE EFFORT...
...SO THAT THIS MIRACLE...
...CAN CONTINUE...
...FOREVER AND EVER.
BECAUSE WALKING TOGETHER...
...HAND IN HAND...
...ISN'T SOME-THING...

...I'LL EVER TAKE FOR GRANTED.
I HAVE NO REGRETS.
SO...
...IF DEATH COMES KNOCKING AT MY DOOR NOW, I WILL BE READY TO GO.
SHE'S RIGHT! THAT'S NOT EVEN FUNNY!!
COMING FROM YOU, THAT'S NOT FUNNY!!
AH-HA-HA!
D-D-D-DON'T TALK LIKE THAT! YOU SHOULDN'T SAY...
...THAT KIND OF THING!
NOW YOU'RE LAUGHING IT OFF!!

COME ON, MASTER... THIS AIN'T THE END...
WE'RE FINALLY AT THE "AND FROM NOW ON" PART...
THAT'S IT! EXACTLY! BESIDES...
HISO (WHISPER)
HISO
HISO
HISO
...if those two get married and have a baby, it'll be your grand-child..!
Your grand-child!!
"Grand-paaa! ♡"
THINK ABOUT IT!!
GRAND...
...PAAA...
...AA...
...AAA!♡
I GUESS I CAN STILL HANG IN THERE FOR A WHILE YET...
I LOOK FORWARD TO IT.
Y...
YES.
I'M LOOKING FORWARD TO IT TOO...?
DOESN'T KNOW WHAT THEY WERE SAYING
WELL, THANK GOODNESS.
PHEW...
HEY...
AHHH!
HAS SOME IDEA
I NEED TO WIPE THE FLOORS...
...SO...

......
RIDICULOUS...
ISUZU-SA—
AH!
HMPH!
TA (TMP)
ISUZU-SAN...
...
WHAT'S EATING HER...?
NOT EVERY-ONE...
...IS IN THE SAME SITUATION.

SHE'S...
...BEEN THROUGH A LOT...
HOW...
...CAN YOU ACT...
...LIKE NOTHING EVER HAPPENED?
SHE DID...
...ALL KINDS OF NASTY STUFF...
...TO KYO.
AND SHE...
...HURT YOU A LOT TOO.
THOSE WOUNDS...
...WILL NEVER DISAPPEAR, WILL THEY!?

IF...
IF I...
...HAD TO DECIDE WHETHER TO FORGIVE OR NOT...
...THEN I WOULDN'T FORGIVE HER.
I CAN'T FORGIVE...!
I'M NOT SAYING I WANT HER TO GET DOWN ON HER KNEES AND BEG FOR IT.
I WOULDN'T EVEN KNOW WHAT TO DO IF SHE DID ACTUALLY APOLOGIZE.
IT'S NOT LIKE THAT.
IT'S NOT ABOUT THAT...
DOES THAT MAKE ME THE BAD GUY?
IS THAT SO WRONG?
HOW IS EVERYONE ELSE OKAY WITH THIS?
WHY IS IT...
...
...THAT NO MATTER WHAT I DO...

SHE'S BEEN THROUGH...
...A LOT...
...AND MANY THINGS...
...ARE OVER NOW.
BUT...
...SO MUCH PAIN...
...REMAINS.
...SORRY, I CAN'T REALLY EXPLAIN IT WELL...
WOUNDS LIKE THAT...
...WON'T JUST SUDDENLY BE WIPED AWAY LIKE MAGIC.
ALL OF THEM...
...THIS MESS IN MY HEART...
...WON'T GO AWAY...?

...MIGHT BE HIDING PAIN DEEP IN THEIR HEARTS...
...PAIN THEY DON'T WANT OTHERS TO SEE.
ISUZU-SAN...
IT'S NOT WRONG.
AND I'M SO THANKFUL...
...THAT YOU'RE FEELING THIS PAIN FOR ME...
...IN MY STEAD.
I'M SO THANKFUL...
...
......
...HARU...
HE'S PROBABLY...
...DISAPPOINTED IN ME, HUH...?

SEEMS LIKE THIS IS ALL I CAN TALK ABOUT...
...THESE DAYS.
GUSHI (SNIFF)
HE MUST HATE ME BY NOW...
OF COURSE HE DOESN'T HATE YOU!!
YOU DON'T KNOW THAT...
I KNOW HIM WELL ENOUGH!! THAT'S JUST OUT OF THE QUESTION!!
GUSHI
GUSHI
HOW CAN YOU BE SO SURE...? KINDA TICKS ME OFF...
OKAY, UNDERSTOOD! I'LL GO ASK HIM! I'LL ASK HATSU-HARU-SAN RIGHT—
DOSHI (WHUD)
NNGH!
HOLD IT, YOU IDIOT! DON'T YOU DARE!!
ARE THEY CLOWNIN' AROUND...?
I THINK...

...THEY'LL NEED TIME.
A WHOLE...
...LOT...
...OF TIME.
I HEAR YOU VISITED REN-SAN AGAIN TODAY.
I UNDER-STAND THAT YOU WEREN'T ABLE TO HAVE MUCH OF A CONVERSATION THOUGH.
I THINK IT WOULD BE MUCH EASIER IF YOU JUST SENT HER PACKING.
...WELL.
PERHAPS THE SITUATION IS MORE COMPLICATED DUE TO...
...YOUR DECISION TO STAY HERE...

BEING YOUNG... MUST BE NICE.
IT SEEMS YOU HAVE NO PROBLEM CHANGING COURSE...
YOU HAVE DRIVE...
...AND STAMINA TOO...
I, ON THE OTHER HAND ......
I WAS BORN IN THE SOHMA COMPOUND AND HAVE LIVED HERE ALL MY LIFE.
LIFE OUTSIDE THESE WALLS...
...IS A COMPLETE MYSTERY TO ME......
BUT I...
NOW THAT I'VE...
...REACHED THIS AGE, IT'S TOO LATE. I'VE SPENT...
...FORTY YEARS...
...FIFTY YEARS...
...SIXTY YEARS... BUILDING MY LIFE HERE.
I...
IT'S TOO LATE FOR ME TO CHANGE IT NOW. I CAN'T CHANGE IT.

...I'M...
...JUST...
...TOO OLD...
...FOR THIS...
IT'S IMPOSSIBLE...
...FOR ME TO CHANGE...
...EVERYTHING...
THAT'S OKAY.
JUST A LITTLE BIT AT FIRST IS FINE.
IF YOU...
...REACH OUT TO ME...

...LIKE YOU LET ME...
...REACH OUT TO YOU...
THE IDEA THAT...

...EVERY-THING WILL BE RIGHT AS RAIN...
...BY TOMORROW OR THE DAY AFTER...
...IS A SAD LIE.
THE VISION ...
...OF EVERY-ONE...
...FEELING GOOD AND BEAMING WITH JOY...
...IS STILL ...
...A FAR-OFF DREAM.
BUT...

...NO MATTER HOW MANY YEARS...
...OR DECADES IT TAKES...
...I WANT TO REACH THAT GOAL.
I WANT TO KEEP WORKING AT IT...
...WITHOUT GIVING UP.
HAAH...
ALL THESE WOMEN SURE LOVE TOHRU, HUH...?
MAYBE THAT'S A DIFFERENT SORT OF PROBLEM...

AND IF ONE DAY THEY'LL BE ABLE TO SMILE FREELY...
...THAT WILL MAKE ME...
...THE HAPPIEST OF ALL.

Chapter 134

MY BEADS ARE IN HER ROOM.
THEY'RE NEXT TO HER MOM NOW.
SHE WON'T THROW 'EM AWAY.
I GET WHERE SHE'S COMING FROM, I GUESS...
THOSE THINGS ...

THEY'RE LIKE PIECES OF HER HEART...
I THINK.
KYO-KUN, KYO-KUN, LOOK OVER HERE!
KYO-KUN!
IT'S A MINI ISUZU-SAN...!
THAT'S A PONY.
LITTLE BITTY THING, AIN'T IT?
GIVE ME SOMETHING!
It's adorable... ♡
I SAID, GIVE ME SOMETHING!
WHERE SHOULD WE HEAD NEXT, KYO-KUN?
THE PATH SPLITS HERE.
HUH? OH YEAH?
WHAT DO YOU WANNA SEE MOST? WE'LL GO THAT WAY.

SIGN: BIRDS
の鳥
THEN—ELEPHANTS! LET'S GO SEE THE ELEPHANTS!
I DON'T SEE ANY GIRAFFES...
I WASN'T ASKIN' FOR THE OPINION OF THE CHAPER-ONES...
DUMBASS. WHAT ARE WE GONNA SEE, IF NOT THE ELEPHANTS?
IF THEY DON'T HAVE 'EM, THEN AT LEAST SHOW ME THE POLAR BEARS!
THERE AREN'T ANY GIRAFFES...
IF YOU'RE JUST GONNA COMPLAIN, GO HOME......
I NEVER GAVE YOU PERMISSION TO TAG ALONG...
AH...
THEY'RE FIGHTING.
DON'T FIGHT!
THIS IS YOUR PROBLEM RIGHT HERE!
BISHI (POINT)
ON A FIRST DATE, YOU'RE SUPPOSED TO TAKE A GIRL TO AN EXCITING PLACE, LIKE AN AMUSEMENT PARK!
UM ...
UH ...
OR AT LEAST A BIGGER ZOO THAN THIS...
WHAT!?
AH-HA!!
DON'T YELL...

THANK
YOU
SO
VERY

I BET YOU'RE AFRAID OF HEIGHTS! YOU'RE ONE OF THOSE GUYS WHO WON'T EVEN RIDE A FERRIS WHEEL, HUH!?
YOU'RE SUCH A BZZZZZ! THAT YOU PROBABLY DON'T EVEN HAVE A BZZZZ!
AAAAAAH!
HOW THE HELL WOULD I KNOW!? I NEVER EVEN BEEN IN ONE OF 'EM! AND DON'T SHOUT WORDS LIKE THAT IN PUBLIC!!
ZAWA
ZAWA (MURMUR)
ZAWA
ZAWA
I DON'T NEED TO GET SEXUALLY HARASSED AT THE ZOO!
AH ...
ELE-PHANTS !!
Kitty-Cat Petting Corner
HISS!
GIRAFFES ...
QUIT YOUR GRUMBLING AND SHOW ME THE DAMN ELEPHANTS ALREADY!
WHAT ARE YOU TWO!? LOAN SHARKS!?
AH...
UM!
IT LOOKS LIKE WE CAN PLAY WITH CATS OVER THERE...

I LIKE ELEPHANTS, BUT CATS ARE GREAT TOO!
OH...
EVEN IF IT'S DIFFICULT TO SQUAT DOWN IN THIS DRESS, I CAN'T HELP BUT PET THE CUTE KITTIES...
SO TIRED...!
UM... UO-CHAN, HANA-CHAN...
OH.
NAH, IT'S NOT THAT.
I ASKED KYO-KUN TO TAKE ME HERE...
...BUT DID YOU TWO... WANT TO GO SOMEWHERE ELSE...?
I ACTUALLY LIKE THIS PLACE. VERY LOW-KEY AND LAIDBACK...
AH...
LET'S GET SOFT SERVE ICE CREAM AFTER THIS!
WE JUST LIKE GIVING HIM A HARD TIME.
I'VE MADE PEACE WITH THE FACT THAT THEY DON'T HAVE GIRAFFES HERE...
ZURU (DRAG) ズル
ZURU ズル
ZURU ズル
ZURU ズル
ZURU ズル
HEY, KYON! HURRY UP, OR WE'RE GONNA LEAVE YOU BEHIND!

OHHH!
KITTIES!
THEY'RE TOO CUTE!
They're adorable...
MEOW!
MEOW!
HUH?
KYON! KYON!
WHAT?
OVER THERE!
......
A BLACK CAT SUITS HER...
ぶし
BUSHIII (GROWL)
THEY HAVE THE SAME SURLY EXPRESSION ......
IT'S LIKE HER FAMILIAR, RIGHT?

HMPH...
...
すとん
SUTON (PLOP)

THAT DAY...
...I WATCHED TOHRU PICK UP...
...MY SCAT-TERED BEADS.
I COULDN'T FIND ANY WORDS TO SAY.

AMONG OTHER THINGS, THEY WERE PROOF OF THE MONSTER I'D BEEN.
I THOUGHT I WOULDN'T HAVE MINDED JUST LEAVING THEM TO ROT...
...BUT AT THE SAME TIME...
...I HAD THIS FEELING THAT SOMEDAY DOWN THE LINE...
...I MIGHT REGRET NOT PICKING THEM UP.
EVEN SO, I COULDN'T MOVE.
SO SHE PICKED 'EM UP INSTEAD.
IT FELT LIKE SHE WAS PROTECTING...
...BOTH THE PRESENT ME AND THE FUTURE ME.

OR MAYBE...
...IT WAS EVEN MORE THAN THAT.
MAYBE SHE WANTED TO PROTECT SOMETHING BIGGER...
MAYBE SHE WAS TRYING TO SAVE ALL THOSE FEELINGS FROM FAR AWAY...
...OF EVERY POOR SOUL WHO HAD TO WEAR A STRING OF PRAYER BEADS JUST SO THEY COULD LIVE THEIR LIVES.
I DON'T HAVE THE ANSWER.
BUT THE ONE THING...
...I DO KNOW...
...IS THAT "LOVE"...
...ISN'T JUST ABOUT LOVING WHAT'S IN FRONT OF YOU.
THE PAST...
THE FUTURE ...

MAYBE IT'S ABOUT HOLDING ALL OF THEM CLOSE TO YOUR HEART.
THAT'S ...
... WHAT I THINK, AT LEAST.
WHEN I LOOK AT HER...

...THAT'S WHAT I THINK.
YUN-YUN, YOU'RE GOING TO A UNIVERSITY THAT FAR AWAY?
YEAH.
THEY HAVE THE MAJOR I'M INTERESTED IN.
I'LL BE LIVING ON MY OWN STARTING THIS SPRING.
HUH?
ARE YOU SERIOUS?
OH, SO YOU'RE A BIG BOY NOW?
CAREFUL— I DON'T WANNA PAY YOU A VISIT SOMETIME AND FIND YOUR CORPSE INSTEAD.

THEY SAY "EXPERIENCE IS THE BEST TEACHER," RIGHT?
DOES CHII-CHAN KNOW ABOUT THIS?
LOOK, MY HEART'S SET ON THIS, SO CUT IT OUT.
So you've finally...
...ascended the stairs to adulthood, I see......
SAY THAT TO MACHI, AND YOU'RE GOING TO GET PUNCHED.
YES, AND SHE'S FINE WITH IT.
I SEE. GOOD...
OH HO HO...!
*"CHII-CHAN" IS HER NICKNAME FOR MACHI
BUT...
...DO YOU KNOW HOW TO FIND A PLACE, AND THINGS LIKE THAT?
WHAT ARE YOU GONNA DO ABOUT A COSIGNER?
YOUR PARENTS?
EVEN THOUGH I KNOW THEY'RE THE LAST PEOPLE YOU WANNA RELY ON...
...I DID CONSIDER THAT...
SO I TALKED TO MY BROTHER...
...BUT THINGS ARE KIND OF UP IN THE AIR AT MY PARENTS' HOUSE RIGHT NOW. IT ISN'T THE TIME TO BE ASKING FOR A FAVOR.
UH-OH!

DON'T TELL ME— LET ME GUESS!
HE WAS TOTALLY PSYCHED ABOUT HELPING YOU OUT!
YEP, YOU GOT THAT RIGHT...
HE LEFT YESTERDAY ON A LITTLE SCOUTING TRIP TO FIND A SUITABLE APARTMENT FOR ME.
HE MOVES FAST!
I'M GRATEFUL TO HIM, OF COURSE, BUT...
BEHOLD, MINE!
ZA (STOMP)
THE CLEAR, BLUE SKY, THE GREEN BUDS OF NATURE...
ALL I CAN SAY IS THERE COULD BE NO FINER PLACE FOR YUKI'S FRESH START!
Agreed!
THEREFORE! I WILL PROCEED WITH MY GUT FEELING AND SHALL NOW PROCLAIM MY COURSE OF ACTION!

I SHALL CONSTRUCT YUKI'S PALACE ON THIS SPOT!!!
Marvelous idea—!
IT MOST CERTAINLY IS NOT A GOOD IDEA! NO ONE CAN LIVE HERE, LET ALONE CONSTRUCT A PALACE!!
LOOK, A MAID! IT'S A MAID!
A MAID AND THE MASTER SHE SERVES!
WHO ARE YOU PEOPLE!?
I HOPE HE LOOKS FOR AN ORDINARY PLACE... BUT I KNOW BETTER.
NOT REALLY DREAMING BIG, ARE YOU?
COME TO THINK OF IT, KAKERU, WHAT ARE YOU DOING...
...ABOUT COLLEGE?
HMM?
I'M GOING.
TO ONE AROUND HERE.
I DIDN'T REALLY WANNA GO, TO BE HONEST.
I INTENDED TO JUST START WORKING AT KOMAKI'S FAMILY BUSINESS AFTER HIGH SCHOOL GRADUATION...
...BUT EVERYONE KEEPS TELLING ME TO GO...
HER FAMILY OWNS A DRY-CLEANER'S

SO, FINE— I GUESS I WILL!
IT'S LIKE THAT.
NOOO, THERE GOES ALL MY SAVINGS...
IF YOU CAN AFFORD TO, YOU SHOULD GO.
BECAUSE YOU'RE SMART...
THINK OF IT LIKE HAVING A LOT OF PART-TIME JOBS! THERE ARE ALL KINDS OF EXPERIENCES YOU CAN ONLY GET FROM COLLEGE...
FIIINE, SINCE YOU PUT IT THAT WAY...
...I'LL CHEAT ON YOU WITH A COED! THAT'S AN EXPERIENCE, RIGHT!?
WHY WOULD YOU SAY THAT...?
IT'S OKAY. I'VE NEVER WORRIED ABOUT THAT A DAY IN MY LIFE.
AREN'T WE JUST STUPIDLY IN LOVE?
YEP, YOU'RE CERTAINLY STUPID.
YOU'RE MORE LIKELY TO CHEAT, YUN-YUN!
I WOULD NOT.
AREN'T YOU GUYS...
...A BIT NERVOUS...? THAT YOU WON'T GET ACCEPTED...
...TO THE COLLEGE OF YOUR CHOICE?

UH, NO?
I... I SEE...
I FEEL LIKE THEIR ANSWER WOULD PISS OFF THOSE STUDENTS WHO ARE ANXIOUSLY PREPARING FOR THEIR OWN ENTRANCE EXAMS...
AHHH!
WE REALLY STRETCHED OUR LEGS TODAY!
BUT IT WAS FUN, WASN'T IT...?
YES, A LOT OF FUN!!
UM...
DO YOU MIND IF I WASH MY HANDS BEFORE WE GO?
YOU OKAY GOING BY YOURSELF?
UGH...
I'M BEAT...
YES... I'LL BE RIGHT BACK!

...ANY-WAY...
ちら
CHIRA (GLANCE)
HOW SHE CAN DRESS LIKE THAT AND NOT BE SWEATING BUCKETS?
IT AIN'T HUMAN...
SHEER WILL-POWER...
WAAAAH!
DON'T GO READIN' MY MIND!!!
WAIT...
SO IT'S LIKE MIND OVER MATTER!? YOU CAN DO ANYTHING WITH WILL-POWER!?
I CAN. I'M LIGHT YEARS AHEAD OF YOU...
LIGHT YEARS...
NAH, IT'S FINE. I DON'T MIND SWEATIN' LIKE A NORMAL PERSON...
...
じろり。
JIRORI (STARE)
WH...
びくり。
BIKURI (TWITCH)
WHAT...?

YOU'RE GOING TO...
...TAKE HER AWAY, AREN'T YOU...?
...YES.
I KNEW ...
...THIS DAY WOULD COME.
I KNEW ...
...WE'D HAVE TO PART WAYS.

BUT...
...
!?
IT'S SELFISH ......
... AH ...
I'M S......
...
B...
BUT I...
RIGHT HERE AND NOW...

...IF YOU CALL ME "MAMA," I'LL FORGIVE YOU...
UH...? THE HECK?
SO I'M GONNA DIE......?
HANAJIMA!
DON'T TEASE HIM SO MUCH!
ALL RIGHT ...
TCH!
SHE JUST SAID "TCH"...!!
LISTEN, KYON. AS MUCH AS WE YANK YOUR CHAIN...
...WE DO LIKE YOU, Y'KNOW?
YOU'RE DUMB, BUT IMPOSSIBLE TO HATE.
YOU'RE A GOOD GUY!

DUMB THOUGH...
YEAH. DUMB THOUGH...
......
TOHRU...
...IS OUR BEST FRIEND...
...OUR COMRADE...
...AND OUR FAMILY.
...IN ALL SERIOUS-NESS...
...WE'RE COUNTING ON YOU.

LEAVE OTOU-SAMA TO ME...
TH...
THAT HAS NOTHIN' TO DO WITH THIS...!
...RIGHT...?
I THINK...?
I'M SORRY I TOOK SO LONG...!
THE LINE WAS REALLY...
...LONG?
BUT WAIT—NO. I CAN'T LET MY EGO GET IN THE WAY OF MASTER'S HAPPINESS. ISN'T IT HIS CHOICE TO DECIDE WHAT MAKES HIM HAPPY? SO IF HE CHOOSES HER, WHO AM I TO COMPLAIN? HUH? WAIT A SECOND. ARE THOSE TWO EVEN THAT FAR ALONG?
H...
HUH? WHERE DID THEY GO?
...THEY WENT HOME.
WHAT!!?
S-SORRY! I KEPT EVERYONE WAITING FOR SO LONG...
NAH, IT WASN'T THAT. DON'T WORRY.
I MEAN, DOES SHE REALLY WANT ME TO CALL HER "MAMA"?
......

UMM!
TOHRU.
THERE'S ONE MORE PLACE I WANNA GO AFTER THIS.
UNLESS YOU DON'T WANNA?
HUH? OH, NO, I DON'T MIND...
WHERE ARE WE GOING?
UM...
I BROUGHT THIS...
...FROM MY PARENTS' HOUSE.
IT'S ONLY MEAT...
...BUT...
...IF YOU'D LIKE IT...

YAY!
THANK YOU, CHII-CHAN! ♥
GOOD THING MACHI DIDN'T TRY TO COOK IT HERSELF—SHE WOULDA BURNED IT!
...SHUT UP.
BUT— I'M GLAD!
I WAS WORRIED YOU WOULDN'T COME.
YOU WERE HESITANT, REMEMBER?
LET'S GO VISIT KAKERU'S HOUSE!
HUH ......?
"I WOULD MUCH RATHER BE ALONE WITH YOU..."
I NEVER SAID THAT!!
YOU SAYING THINGS LIKE THAT IS EXACTLY WHY I DIDN'T WANT TO COME!!
You've ascended the stairs to adult-hood......

I DID WARN YOU......
THE MEAT —!!!
HUH?
THAT'S ALL YOU'RE WORRIED ABOUT!?
......
I MENTIONED THIS...
...BEFORE...
...SO I WANNA...
...GET THE REST OUT.

I...
AFTER I GRADUATE ...
...I'VE BEEN THINKIN' THAT I WANNA GET AWAY FROM HERE.
本田家
GRAVESTONE: HONDA FAMILY
AH...
NOT LIKE THAT. NOT IN A WEIRD WAY.
IT'S NOT LIKE I'M BEING PESSIMISTIC OR TRYING TO RUN AWAY.
IT'S JUST— UP TO NOW, I'VE BEEN...
...AVOIDIN' THE WORLD... LIVING MY LIFE LIKE I WAS SOMEHOW APART FROM IT.
I WAS BEING SELFISH, AND MOST OF THE PEOPLE AROUND ME DIDN'T CARE TO CORRECT THAT.

BUT THINGS ARE DIFFERENT NOW.
I'M A NORMAL HUMAN BEING...
...AND AS A NORMAL HUMAN BEING...
...I CAN FINALLY...
...BE WITH YOU IN THIS WORLD.
THAT MAKES ME...
...SO HAPPY...
SO, MORE AND MORE...
...I WANT TO BE A PART OF THIS WORLD.
I WANT TO PUT MYSELF...
...TO THE TEST...
...SOME-PLACE I'VE NEVER BEEN BEFORE...!

......
AND IF POSSI-BLE...
...I'D LIKE TO DO THAT...
...WITH YOU BY MY SIDE.
本

Chapter 135

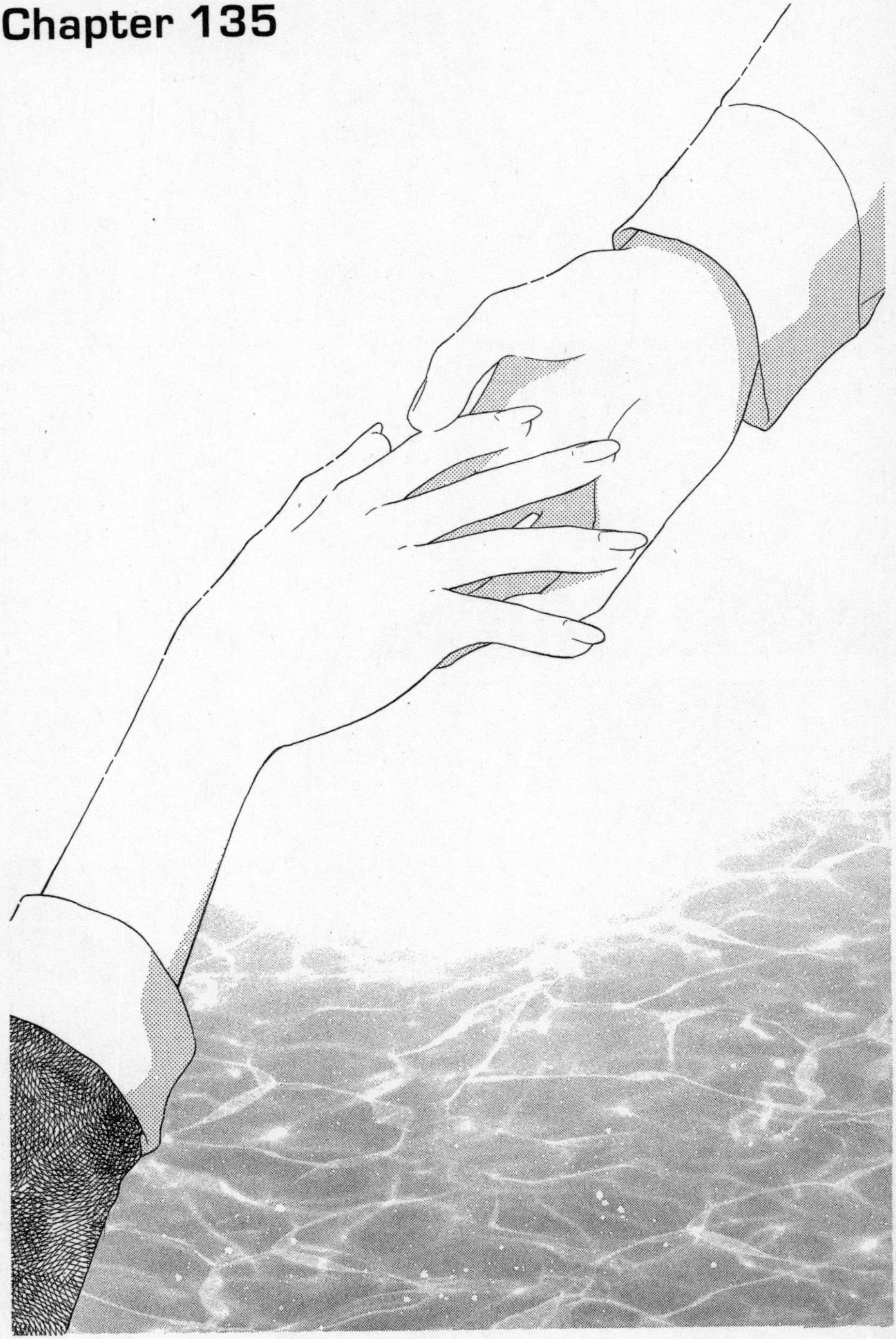

......
YOU WANT...
...TO LEAVE HERE...
...AND GO... WHERE...?
本田家

WELL, MASTER ...
...
THE TRUTH IS...
...I TRIED TO FIND SOMEPLACE ON MY OWN, WITHOUT RELYING ON ANYONE...
...BUT HE WOULDN'T LET ME.
... MASTER ...
...HAS AN ACQUAIN-TANCE...
...WHO HAS A DOJO...
...FAR, FAR AWAY FROM HERE.

I COULD WORK...
...AND LEARN THERE AT THE SAME TIME.
THAT WOULD REALLY HELP, I THINK.
GETTING MORE LIFE EXPERIENCE IN THE OUTSIDE WORLD.
SO THEN SOMEDAY...
...WHEN I INHERIT MASTER'S DOJO...
...I'LL BE ABLE TO USE WHAT I LEARNED.
ALL OF IT...

BOTH THE GOOD...
...AND THE BAD.
......
I KNOW...
本田家
...THAT SOUNDS...
...A BIT CHILDISH.
AND I KNOW IT'S SELFISH, WANTING TO TAKE YOU AWAY FROM...
...ALL THE PEOPLE WHO LOVE YOU.
I KNOW THAT.
BUT I CAN'T KEEP...
...LYING TO MYSELF... ANYMO—
YES.

THERE'S NO NEED FOR YOU TO DECEIVE YOURSELF.
...MASTER-SAN...
...WAS PLEASED, WASN'T HE?
WHEN YOU ASKED HIM ABOUT THIS.
HUH ...?
YEAH...... I GUESS HE WAS.
...THIS MAY SOUND CONCEITED ...
...BUT I THINK...
...I ALSO...
...UNDER-STAND THAT FEELING.
WHEN KYO-KUN...

...TALKS ABOUT "THE FUTURE"...
WHEN HE SHOWS SUCH...
...A STRONG DESIRE TO LIVE...
AND IT MAKES ME HAPPY.
...IT MAKES ME HAPPY.
THAT'S WHY...
...WE'LL BOTH GO.
TOGETHER ...!

HUH ...?
WHAT !!?
A...
ARE YOU SURE...!? YOU KNOW WHAT I'M ASKIN', RIGHT!?
IT'S, LIKE, REALLY FAR AWAY! YOU WON'T BE ABLE TO SEE EVERYBODY ELSE WHENEVER YOU WANT, LIKE HERE!
AND, UH, WE'RE NOT EXACTLY GONNA BE LIVING IN THE LAP OF LUXURY...
ALTHOUGH I'LL DO MY DAMNED BEST!!
?
YOU'RE THE ONE WHO ASKED ME TO GO WITH YOU, KYO-KUN...
Y-YEAH, I KNOW, BUT... HOW CAN I PUT IT...
I DIDN'T EXPECT YOU TO GIVE ME AN ANSWER RIGHT AWAY!
LIKE, IF YOU NEED MORE TIME TO THINK ABOUT IT, THAT'S COOL WITH ME! AND IF YOU DON'T LIKE THE IDEA, YOU CAN JUST SAY SO!
I KNOW I SEEM LIKE A PUSHOVER, BUT YOU'D BE HARD-PRESSED TO FORCE ME TO ACCEPT SOMETHING LIKE THIS IF I DIDN'T WANT IT TOO.
I CAN BE PRETTY STUBBORN.
HEH HEH!
YEAH... YOU'RE DEFINITELY STUBBORN WHEN YOU WANT TO BE...
EXACTLY.
I MADE UP MY OWN MIND.
...THAT'S WHY I WANT TO...
...TELL YOU ONE MORE THING.

MOM DOESN'T HOLD A GRUDGE AGAINST YOU, KYO-KUN.
本田家
EVEN IF SHE REALLY DID SAY...
...SHE WOULD NEVER FORGIVE YOU...
...I'M SURE IT WASN'T OUT OF HATRED.
I'M POSITIVE ABOUT THAT.
I'M ABSOLUTELY POSITIVE.

...SO THIS IS ME...
... STANDING MY GROUND.
I'M STAYING WITH YOU, KYO-KUN.
WE'LL GO TOGETHER.
IT'S TRUE, LEAVING EVERYONE...
...WILL BE QUITE SAD.
BUT IF YOU LEFT ME BEHIND, KYO-KUN...
...THAT WOULD BE SO MUCH WORSE.
I WANT TO ALWAYS...
...BE BY YOUR SIDE.
I DON'T WANT TO BE SEPARATED FROM YOU.
I DON'T WANT TO SIT HERE WAITING FOR YOU.

SO PLEASE— TAKE ME WITH YOU.

THAT'S OKAY, RIGHT?
......
...I'LL TAKE HER WITH ME.
I PROMISE...
...TO PROTECT HER.
THANK YOU...
IT... TOOK ME WAY TOO LONG, BUT...
本田

...I'LL PROTECT HER...
...FOR THE REST OF MY LIFE.
...
THAT WORKS, RIGHT?

ザァァ…
ZAAA (RUSTLE)
...NO, STOP!

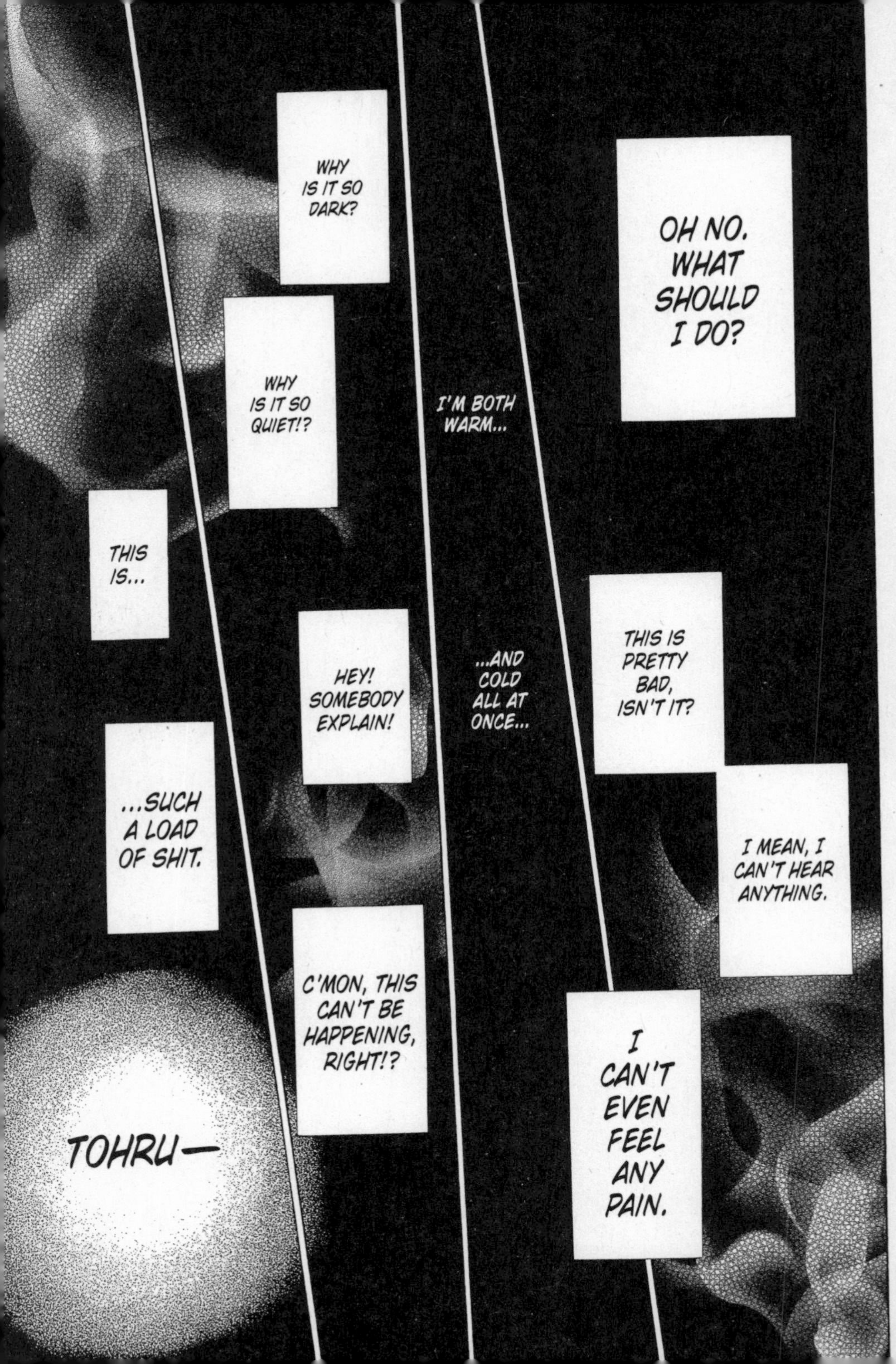
OH NO. WHAT SHOULD I DO?
THIS IS PRETTY BAD, ISN'T IT?
I MEAN, I CAN'T HEAR ANYTHING.
I CAN'T EVEN FEEL ANY PAIN.
I'M BOTH WARM...
...AND COLD ALL AT ONCE...
WHY IS IT SO DARK?
WHY IS IT SO QUIET!?
HEY! SOMEBODY EXPLAIN!
C'MON, THIS CAN'T BE HAPPENING, RIGHT!?
THIS IS...
...SUCH A LOAD OF SHIT.
TOHRU—

I THINK...
...I'M DYING.
WHAT SHOULD I DO?
I NEVER THOUGHT...
...IT WOULD END LIKE THIS.
WHAT SHOULD I DO? I HATE THIS.
I DON'T WANT TO DIE LIKE THIS.
I DON'T WANT TO DIE!
TOHRU...

SHE'LL BE ALL ON HER OWN.
I CAN'T LEAVE HER.
WE CAN'T PART LIKE THIS.
WHAT'S GOING TO HAPPEN TO HER...
...IF I'M NOT THERE?
SHE JUST STARTED HIGH SCHOOL...
SHE'S STILL A CHILD.
SHE...
SHE'S STILL...

KAZUYA.
I...
...UNDERSTAND NOW.
LEAVING SOMEONE BEHIND, BEING LEFT BEHIND...
BOTH OF THEM...
...ARE HEART-BREAKING, AREN'T THEY?
...I'M SORRY.
I'M SORRY.
I'M SORRY, TOHRU. YOU AT LEAST KNEW...
...I LOVED YOU, RIGHT?
TOHRU...
I WANTED TO...

...LOVE YOU EVEN MORE.
...
HEY ......
ANYBODY, PLEASE...
SOME-BODY...
PROTECT THAT GIRL.
SHE'S NOT VERY GOOD AT...
...CRYING FOR HERSELF...
...BUT EVEN SO, IF SHE DOES CRY...
...YOU HAVE TO STAY WITH HER.
SOMEBODY, PLEASE...
HEY, SOME-BODY...
SHE'S MY TREASURE.
PROTECT HER...
SOME-BODY...
ANY-BODY...

EVEN IF YOU'VE...
...FORGOTTEN ALL ABOUT ME...
IF YOU MEET HER...
...PLEASE REMEMBER.
PLEASE...
THE NEXT TIME SHE GETS LOST...
...I WANT YOU TO FIND HER.
PLEASE...
EVEN JUST ONCE WOULD BE FINE...
YOU......
......

YOU HAVE TO...
...KEEP YOUR PROMISE, OR...
...I'LL NEVER...
...FORGIVE YOU......
PLEASE...
PLEASE...
I'M BEGGING YOU...
PLEASE DO WHAT I CAN'T ANY LONGER...

PROTECT HER!
FEELS LIKE...
...I'M SINKING...
LIKE EVERYTHING'S SHUTTING DOWN...
......OH.
I'M SORRY.
...PLEASE...
LOOKS LIKE THIS IS GOOD-BYE.

...LET TOHRU HAVE A HAPPY LIFE.
AN AMBULANCE...!
HAS SOMEONE CALLED FOR AN AMBULANCE!?
IT LOOKS LIKE THE DRIVER IS UNCONSCIOUS TOO...
HANG IN THERE!
PLEASE LET HER BE LOVED...
...BY MANY PEOPLE.
CAN YOU HEAR ME!? HANG IN THERE!!
STAY WITH ME...
EVEN IF SHE GETS LOST...
EVEN IF SHE MAKES MISTAKES...
IN THE END...
SO MUCH BLOOD...
STAY WITH ME!!
...LET HER LIVE A LIFE SHE CAN BE PROUD OF.
THE KIND OF LIFE...
...THAT'LL MAKE PEOPLE SAY...
..."YOU DID YOUR BEST."

JOYOUS TIMES... SAD TIMES...
THE CYCLE REPEATING ITSELF, AGAIN AND AGAIN.
HANG IN...
THAT'S HOW I WANT...
...HER TO GROW OLDER.
...!
...IT'S TOO LATE.
SHE'S GONE ....

ZAAN
(SPLASH)

ZAN

ZAAN
(SPLASH)

YOU DID YOUR BEST.

The Final Chapter

ON THE DAY OF THE GRADUATION CEREMONY, NO ONE COULD COMPLAIN ABOUT THE WEATHER.
IT WAS A FINE DAY, WITH A LIGHT BREEZE AND BEAUTIFUL CLOUDS FLOATING BY OVERHEAD...
IT WAS AS IF THE DAY WAS CELEBRATING...
...OUR GRADUATION AND THE BEGINNING OF OUR NEW LIVES.
...THAT'S RIGHT.
KYU (SQUEAK)
キュッ
THAT DOES IT!
...ALL RIGHT.

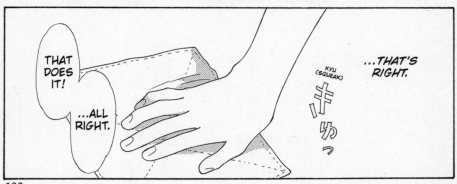

WITH THAT, THE ROOM IS CLEAN ONCE MORE!
YOU REALLY EMPTIED IT OUT, HUH?
YES...
ME AND KYO-KUN'S...
...NEW BEGINNING TOO!
YOUR ROOM IS EMPTY TOO, KYO-KUN.
YEAH, WELL, I GOT NOTHIN' TO LEAVE BEHIND.
BESIDES, WE'RE STAYIN' AT MASTER'S PLACE TONIGHT.
...
THIS KIND OF...
...REMINDS ME OF THE DAY...
...I FIRST MOVED IN HERE.

...YOU CAME CRASHING THROUGH THE—
AAAAAAH!!
THAT'S ALL IN THE......
...PAST...
YES, IT IS!!
I WAS SHOCKED...
...AND THEN EVEN MORE SO WHEN ALL THREE OF YOU TRANS-FORMED.
YUKI-KUN AND SHIGURE-SAN...
...WERE BOTH SO KIND.
BUT I WAS SO NERVOUS.
AND THEN...
BUT IT WAS...
...A LOT OF FUN TOO.

I HAD...
...SO MUCH FUN.
MY DAYS SPENT HERE WITH EVERYONE...
...WERE SO PRECIOUS, THEY'RE LIKE JEWELS.
THEY'RE SO DEAR...
SO VERY DEAR TO ME.
......
I MISS THEM ALREADY.
...I KNEW I WOULD.

AM I MISSING THEM...
... BECAUSE I LOVE THE DAYS WE SPENT TOGETHER ?
I MISS THEM.
I LOVE THEM SO MUCH.
I LOVE THEM...
...SO I MISS THEM IN EQUAL MEASURE.
...YOU DON'T GET IT.
YOU...

YOU...
MORE THAN YOU KNOW...
... EVERY-ONE...
...
...LOVES YOU TOO.
SO...
...IT'S GONNA BE OKAY. IT'S NOT LIKE WE'RE LEAVING FOREVER.
...THIS IS JUST THE BEGINNING ...
...OF A NEW BANQUET.
...RIGHT?

RIGHT!!
GUUUU (GRUMBLE)
I...
I-I-I'M SORRY...!!
...Y'KNOW, YOU GET EMBARRASSED OVER THE WEIRDEST THINGS...

WHAT DO YOU SAY WE GET A SNACK?
...GOOD IDEA!
OH, THAT'S RIGHT.
I WANTED TO GIVE YOU THIS.
...?
THE KEY TO MY NEW PLACE.
COME OVER ANYTIME YOU WANT.
I'D HATE FOR YOU TO WORRY THAT I MAY BE CHEATING ON YOU.
I...
I DON'T ESPECIALLY ...
...WORRY ABOUT... THAT.

THANK
YOU
SO
VERY
MUCH!

GARA (RATTLE)
ガラ
JYA (WHOOSH)
じゃっ
I LIED!!!
Humans are at their best when they're sincere.
HEH HEH...
HEH HEH HEH HEH...
...YOU'RE A JERK...
GU (GRIP)
GU
GU
GU
THAT WAS A JERK MOVE...
...UM...
BUT YOU'VE GOT... A LITTLE MORE TIME...
...BEFORE YOU LEAVE, RIGHT?
YEAH. A BIT.

YOU'RE LEAVING ...
...TOMORROW ......
...WILL YOU MISS THIS?
HMM?
... YEAH.
OF COURSE ...
...I WILL.
......
I MISS IT ALREADY.
JUST THE THOUGHT OF...
...NOT BEING ABLE TO...
...SEE YOU EASILY, YUKI-SENPAI...
SO...
...SO...
...WILL I.

...I'M GOING TO RUN AFTER YOU.
I SWEAR ...
...I'LL CATCH UP TO YOU.
...I'LL BE WAITING.
草摩

NAMEPLATE: SOHMA

OH YEAH, KAGURA-CHAN!
DID YOU KNOW SHIGURE-NIISAN QUIT BEING A NOVELIST?
WHAAT!?
FOR REAL!? I HADN'T HEARD THAT!!
I KNEW HE'S MOVING BACK TO THE COMPOUND, BUT...WHOA. THAT'S A BIG DEAL...
MITSURU-SAN TOLD ME...AND YOU KNOW HER...
SHE WAS PLEASED, TO SAY THE LEAST.
HE'S DESTROYED! THE EVIL ONE HAS BEEN DESTROYED!
I'M HAPPY FOR YOU!
I'M SO HAPPY FOR YOU!
...HMM...
YOU THINK THEY'LL GET MARRIED?
I SUPPOSE IT'S BECAUSE HE'S WITH AKITO NOW.
I CAN'T TELL IF IT WAS A COLD OR PASSIONATE DECISION.
I DUNNO...
SPEAKING OF WHICH...
...WHEN ARE YOU AND MITSURU-SAN GETTING MARRIED, RITSU?
WHA...!!?

M-M-M-M-MARRIED!? I-I DON'T... I MEAN, I-I'M STILL... AFTER ALL, Y-YOU KNOW HOW I AM!
WOULD SHE ACCEPT IT...?
DON'T RIP THE KIMONO! I THOUGHT YOU WERE GIVING IT TO ME!?
WHOAAAAA!
FINE, WHATEVER. DO WHAT YOU WANT.
I'M TIRED OF ALL YOU LOVEBIRDS!
AND I'M NOT JEALOUS! RIGHT NOW, I'M HAVING A LOT OF FUN AT WORK.
I'M BUSY TOO...
HUH...? BUT...
...YOU'RE GOING TO SEE THEM OFF TOMORROW, AREN'T YOU?
WELL, SURE, BUT NOT FOR TOHRU-KUN'S SAKE.
...
I HOPE... THEY'LL BE HAPPY, YOU KNOW...?
IT'S FOR CUTIE KYO-KUN'S SAKE.
NOPE, WRONG!

THAT HOUSE...
EVERYONE'S MOVING OUT... SO I WONDER WHAT WILL HAPPEN TO IT...
ARE THEY GOING TO... TEAR IT DOWN...?
I HEARD THEY'RE GONNA LET IT BE FOR THE TIME BEING.
REALLY ...!?
I KNOW FOR SURE...
...THEY'LL BE HAPPY.

FRUITS BASKET

THAT'S GOOD...
IT'D BE NICE IF SOMEBODY MOVES IN SO THEY DON'T TEAR IT DOWN.
YEAH...
ぽろ PORO (DRIP)
ぽろ PORO
ぽろ PORO
WAA!
WHAT!?
HUH!?
I...
I'M SORRY. IT'S NOTHING...
IT'S JUST— TOMORROW'S SO SOON.
...DON'T WORRY.
I'LL BE ABLE TO SMILE... WHEN WE SEE THEM OFF TOMORROW ......

...THERE'S NO NEED.
...YOU LOVE HER.
YOU GO AHEAD AND CRY TOMORROW TOO.
CRY YOUR EYES OUT.
AFTER ALL...

I HEAR...
...TORI-NII SAID HE WAS SO SURE SOMEONE WAS GONNA SOCK SENSEI IN THE JAW AT SOME POINT.
AND SENSEI JUST GRINNED AND SAID, "BUT IT ALL WORKED OUT, DIDN'T IT?"
OF COURSE NO ONE DID!
WE'VE ALL BECOME MUCH MORE MATURE THAN SHII-CHAN, AFTER ALL!
JIIIN (GLOW)
YEAH...... WE'RE ALL ADULTS NOW...
...
MORE THAN THAT...
...I CAN'T BELIEVE KYO'S TAKING TOHRU AWAY!
I BET HE JUST WANTS TO HAVE HER ALL TO HIMSELF!
I'D LIKE TO GIVE KYO A GOOD PINCH!
HE'D GO, "EEEYOW!"
WHY DON'T YOU PINCH HIM TOMORROW ...?
HUUUH? I COULDN'T DO THAT IN FRONT OF TOHRU!
OH YEAH. BUT THANKS TO HIM, I GOT ANOTHER DREAM.

EVENTUALLY, I'LL FIND MY OWN FABULOUS SWEET-HEART...
...AND I'LL GET TO VISIT THEM AND SHOW OFF HOW HAPPY WE ARE.
SO...
...TOHRU JUST HAS TO BE HAPPY.
FROM HERE ON OUT TOO...
...SHE CAN'T LOSE HER SMILE.

...I THINK...
...SHE SHOULD BREAK UP WITH HIM......
OOH, SOME-BODY'S MAD.
SOME-BODY'S SULKING ...

I...
I AM NOT SULKING...
NOW YOU'RE BLUSH-ING!
...
IT SOUNDS LIKE THEY'RE HAVING A FUN TIME.
YES... VERY MUCH SO...
LISTEN ....
I KNOW I'M THE ONE WHO SUGGESTED YOU HIRE A COOK IN THE FIRST PLACE...
...BUT ARE YOU SURE THIS IS THE RIGHT PERSON...
...FOR THE JOB?
I MEAN, NOT THAT THERE'S ANYTHING WRONG WITH SAKI-SAN! BUT YOU SAW HOW KYO REACTED...
HE WAS WHITE AS A GHOST...
I HIRED HER!
NICE TO MEET YOU. I'M SAKI HANAJIMA.
OH...?
DID YOU SAY SOME-THING...?
NO!! NOT A WORD!!

I'M SORRY. IT'S BEYOND ME. SHE'S HERE TO STAY, KYO...
ALTHOUGH— IS IT JUST ME, OR DOES IT SEEM LIKE THERE'S SOMETHING BETWEEN THEM?
...SO TOMORROW...
...IS THE BIG DAY, HMM?
YES...
...BUT.
AS MUCH AS I'LL MISS THEM...
...I'M NOT WORRIED.
NEITHER AM I...

...HUH ...?
THAT'S RIGHT.
TOMOR-ROW.
I'LL TELL HER YOU WISH HER WELL.
...WELL, SURE. I'LL MISS HER...
...BUT...
...I'M HAPPY FOR THEM. AND I'M KIND OF EXCITED, MYSELF...
...FOR THE JOURNEY.
...Tell me, are the...
...cherry blossoms in bloom there yet?
...Al-most.
Then... I guess I'm almost ready to go on a journey too.
There better be a delicious meal waiting for me!

TORORO SOBA?
AYA-KUN! AYA-KUN!
BUASA (RUSTLE)

How about this one too!!?
AS A GIFT FOR TOHRU-KUN!!
GOOD JOB, MINE!
COLLECT ALL THE DRESSES THAT REALLY SPEAK TO YOU OR MAKE YOU THINK OF HER AND THROW THEM INTO THE BOX!! AFTER ALL, THE BURDEN RESTS ON OUR SHOULDERS TO ENSURE THEY LEAD A GLAMOROUS LIFESTYLE!!
...
BUT, AYA-KUN...
I'VE BEEN IN A SIMILAR SITUATION BEFORE...
...AND IT'S ALWAYS A LITTLE SAD WHEN A CHILD LEAVES THE NEST, ISN'T IT? WE'LL MISS HER.
OF COURSE WE'LL MISS HER!
THAT'S WHY ADULTS PACK BOXES...
...FULL OF CUP NOODLES, SHOES, MAID UNIFORMS—AND SO ON AND SO FORTH—WITH SO MUCH LOVE THAT IT'S ANNOYING...
...AND THEN SEND IT TO THEIR LOVED ONES IN LIEU OF THEIR FEELINGS!

FOR THAT CHILD'S SAKE...
...I WOULD TRAVEL ANYWHERE!
THAT'S EXACTLY WHY...
...WE MUST ALSO SEND YUKI A RIDICULOUS AMOUNT OF "CONGRATULATIONS!" CARE PACKAGES!!
How's this for your little brother!?
THIS KIND OF DRESS WOULD STILL LOOK GOOD ON HIM, WOULDN'T IT!?
PERHAPS EVEN WEEKLY!

OKI-NAWA!?
FOR SUMMER VACATION!? SURE, I'LL GO! LET'S GO!
WAIT, ARE YOU SURE? CAN YOU GET TIME OFF?
YES, THAT'S WHY I INVITED YOU.
WE HAVEN'T BEEN ON A DECENT VACATION YET.
THERE ARE STILL PLENTY OF AREAS IN THIS COUNTRY THAT I'VE NEVER BEEN TO.
I WANT TO START IN THE SOUTH AND VISIT THEM ONE BY ONE...
SOUNDS GOOD TO ME!!
HYUCK! HYUCK!
HAW! HAW!
I LOVE THE IDEA OF YOU DOING SOMETHING THAT TOTALLY DOESN'T SUIT YOU, HATORI-KUN!!
YOU ON A SOUTHERN ISLAND!! YOU WEARING A T-SHIRT!!
HEE HEE!
IT LOOKS LIKE YOU'RE HAVING FUN, MAYU.
KEEP IT UP, AND I WON'T TAKE YOU...
AH!
I CAN'T HELP IT! I CAN'T EVEN IMAGINE YOU WEARING A SWIMSUIT...
I'M NOT GOING TO WEAR A SWIMSUIT.

SORRY, NEVER MIND. I JUST REALIZED THAT I WOULD LOOK EVEN MORE OUT OF PLACE WEARING A SWIMSUIT.
?
WHY?
...WELL, AFTER ALL...
...MY BODY ISN'T... UM...
I'M......
...FLAT, YOU KNOW?
ALL I'VE GOT IS MY HEIGHT...
YOU KNOW ...
HEH HEH HEH
...IT'S A LITTLE LATE TO BE WORRIED ABOUT THAT...
HEH HEH...
I KNOW!! I KNOW, BUT...
YOU CAN LAUGH, BUT... NO, DON'T LAUGH!!
GATA (RATTLE)
ガタッ
LOOK, ANYWAY!!
LET'S CHECK OUT SOME TRAVEL AGENCIES TODAY!!
YOU'RE GOING TO SEE THEM OFF TOMORROW, AREN'T YOU?
YES.

......
I HOPE IT'LL BE A NICE DAY.
YES.
...
OKAY...

NOW THAT ALL OUR BUSINESS IS TAKEN CARE OF...
...WHY DON'T WE STOP SOMEWHERE FUN?
...WE'RE GOING HOME AND WORKING.
YOU'RE SO SERIOUS...
YOU'RE GOING TO SEE THEM OFF TOMORROW, SHIGURE...
...SO WE HAVE TO DO WHATEVER WE CAN TODAY.
YOU'RE REALLY NOT GOING?
...NO, I'M NOT.
IT SHOULD BE FINE FOR YOU TO GO...
...IF YOU WANT TO SEE HER.
...I CAN ALWAYS GO FOR A VISIT.
...INCI-DENTALLY, WHEN YOU DO...
...I SUPPOSE I'LL BE EXPECTED TO COME ALONG TOO, HMM?

...
YOU'RE A CRAFTY GIRL.

KARARA (RATTLE)
カララ…
ZAAA (SHHH)
ザー…
BATAN (SHUT)
バタン
...
HEY.
...ARE YOU DONE...
...CLEANING OUT YOUR THINGS?
PRETTY MUCH.
...THERE'S STILL SOME DINNER LEFT IN THE KITCHEN, SO GO HAVE SOME IF YOU WANT.
KYO.

I'D LIKE TO...
...SPEAK TO HONDA-SAN ALONE.
...IF IT'S OKAY?
...
LIVING ROOM.
HEY.
YOU BETTER DO YOUR BEST OUT THERE...
...YOU STUPID CAT.

...MIND YOUR OWN DAMN BUSI-NESS...
...YOU STUPID RAT.
カラ
KARA (SLIDE)

YUKI-KUN...!
WELCOME HOME!
...I'M HOME.
SO...
...TOMORROW'S THE DAY, RIGHT?
YES!
...
I WON'T...
...GET TO HEAR YOU SAY...
..."WELCOME HOME" TO ME ANYMORE, WILL I, HONDA-SAN?

... BUT ...
BUT I'M...
...HAPPY FOR YOU TOO.
THE "ME" WHO'S ARRIVED AT THIS POINT...
...IS HAPPY FOR YOU.
...... I...
I WAS AL- WAYS ...
...SO WEAK...
I WASN'T GOOD AT MAKING CONNECTIONS WITH OTHER PEOPLE, BUT I WANTED TO BE LOVED.
I WANTED TO BE NEEDED.
I YEARNED FOR THOSE THINGS...

AND THEN, ONE DAY...
...YOU CAME INTO MY LIFE.
YOU...
...MADE THOSE DREAMS COME TRUE...
YOU GRANTED ...
...MY WISHES ...
...WITHOUT ASKING FOR ANYTHING IN RETURN.
...YOU DON'T REALIZE, DO YOU?
YOU'VE ALWAYS...
...BEEN SAVING ME.
YOU GAVE ME SO MUCH.
THANK YOU...
...FOR ALWAYS...

YOU HELPED ME BECOME ...
...A FULL-FLEDGED "HUMAN BEING."
YOU HELPED ME GROW AS A PERSON...
...ACCEPTING MY WEAKNESS.
...AND IT'S...
...BECAUSE OF THAT...
...THAT I CAN STAND IN FRONT OF YOU HERE TODAY.
YOU... WERE LIKE...
...A MOTHER ...
...TO ME.

...
...I WAS FINALLY...
...ABLE TO TELL YOU THAT...
I KNOW MY TRUE FEELINGS...
...ARE A LITTLE...
...ON THE EMBARRASS-ING SIDE...
N—
BUT, YOU KNOW...
...IT'S THE SAME FOR THEM TOO...
...I THINK.
YOUR PRESENCE IS SO WARM...
...AND KIND...

SO...
...EVEN THOUGH WE'RE ALL GOING...
...OUR SEPARATE WAYS NOW, STARTING NEW LIVES IN NEW PLACES...
"IS SHE DOING WELL?"
"SHE'S NOT CRYING, IS SHE?"
"IS SHE...
"...SMILING EVEN NOW?"
...EVERY SO OFTEN, WE'LL STILL...
"IS SHE..."
...THINK OF YOU.

"...HAPPY TODAY TOO?"
THAT'S HOW...
...WE THINK OF YOU.
THAT'S HOW WE'LL ALWAYS THINK OF YOU.
EVERYONE...
...LOVES YOU TOO!

THANK YOU...
I'M SO GLAD...
...I MET YOU.
...
I'M...
...SO GLAD YOU WERE HERE.

THANK YOU...
THANK YOU.
...THANK YOU...
...TOHRU.

THANK YOU.

WELL, HERE WE GO!

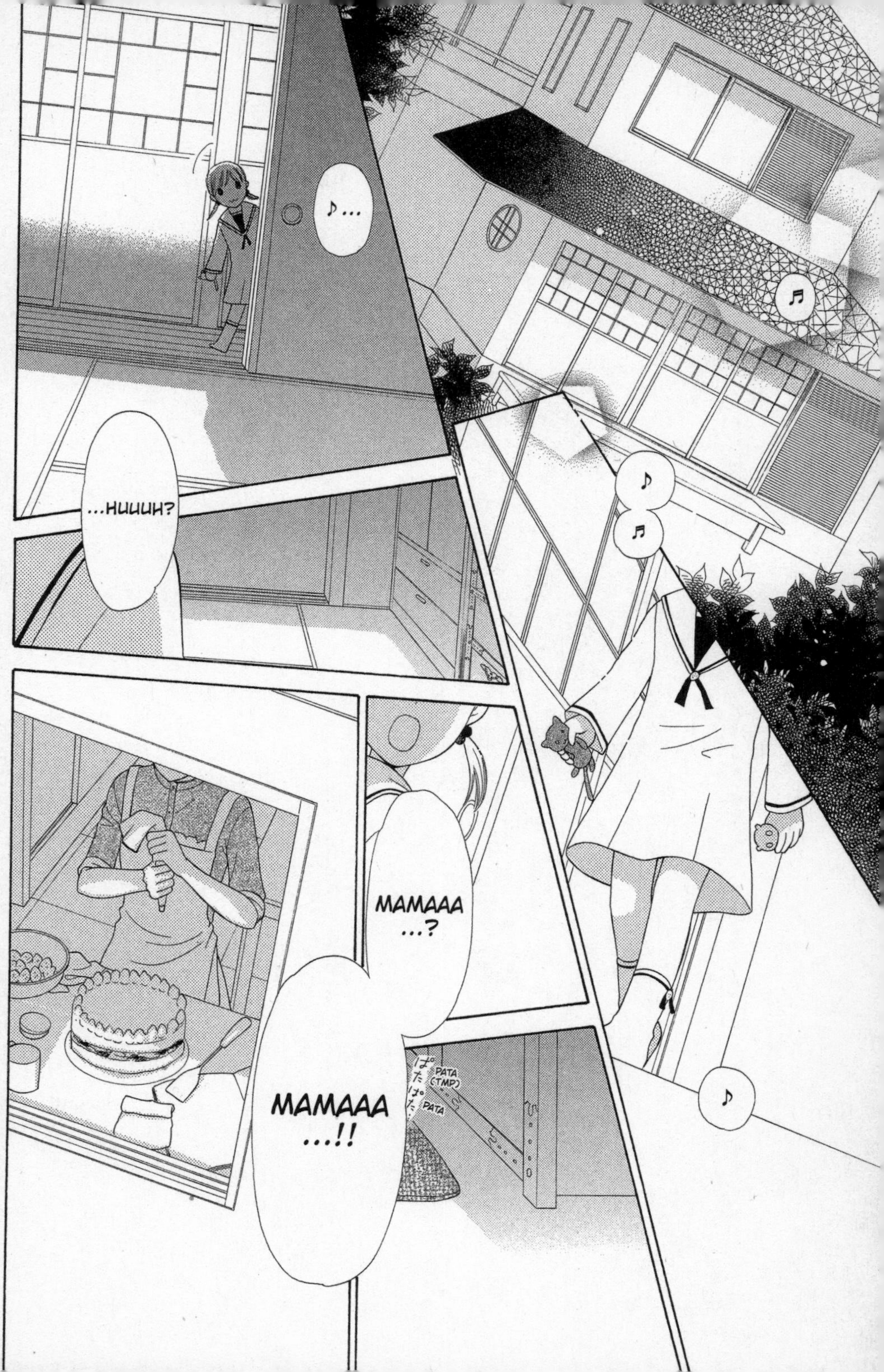
♬
♪
♬
♪
♪...
...HUUUH?
MAMAAA ...?
ぱたぱた PATA (TMP) PATA
MAMAAA ...!!

WHERE'S TOHRU-KUN AND KYO-KUN?
HEY, KNOCK THAT OFF!
YOU SHOULD CALL THEM GRANDMA AND GRANDPA!
HUH?
BUT TOHRU-KUN TOLD ME I COULD CALL HER BY HER NAME!
IF YOU'RE LOOKING FOR GRANDMA AND GRANDPA...
...THEY WENT FOR A WALK.
AWWW...
THEY LEFT ME BEHIND AGAIN!
DON'T INTERRUPT THEIR PRIVATE LOVEY-DOVEY TIME, HONEY.
LOVEY-DOVEY, LOVEY-DOVEY! THEY'RE SO LUCKY!
THEY'RE ALWAYS LIKE THAT!
LET'S WALK TOGETHER ...

...HAND IN HAND.

THROUGH THE JOYOUS TIMES...AND THE SAD...
THE CYCLE REPEATING ITSELF, AGAIN AND AGAIN.
THAT'S HOW...

...WE'LL
GROW OLD
TOGETHER.

Once more, for the last time...

I am deeply grateful
to everyone who read *Fruits Basket*...
to everyone who is reading it now too...
to everyone who picked up this collector's edition...
to everyone who took part in anything to do with *Furuba*.

If I was able to leave behind even one thing, that would make me happy. Thank you so very much.

高屋奈月。
NATSUKI TAKAYA

THEATER FROM THE VAULT

• Contents Details 1 •

Preview cut from Issue 15, 1998 of *Hana to Yume*

♥ Bonus Preview Manga, Part 1 ♥

Published in Issue 15, 1998 of *Hana to Yume*
(Included in *Hana to Yume Comics*, Volume 3)

A preview that announced *Fruits Basket* was starting in the next issue, 16.

×××××××××××××××××××××××××××××××××

♥ Bonus Preview Manga, Part 2 ♥

Published in Issue 22, 1998 of *Hana to Yume*
(Included in *Hana to Yume Comics*, Volume 3)

After Chapter 6 (Issue 21), the author took a one-month break. This preview manga announced that the series would resume the next month, in Issue 23.

×××××××××××××××××××××××××××××××××

♥ Bonus Preview Manga, Part 3 ♥

Published in Issue 5, 1999 of *Hana to Yume*
(Included in *Hana to Yume Comics*, Volume 3)

After Chapter 12 (Issue 4), the author took a one-month break. This preview manga announced that the series would resume the next month, in Issue 6.

×××××××××××××××××××××××××××××××××

♥ Side Story ♥

Published in Issue 5, 1999 of *Hana to Yume*
(Included in *Hana to Yume Comics*, Volume 4)

A short side story that announced the contents of the free *Special CD Set*.

×××××××××××××××××××××××××××××××××

THE END OF THE CENTURY DRAWS NEAR...
A CERTAIN PROPHET PREDICTED THE WORLD'S DESTRUCTION IN 1999... WHO SAYS THE COUNTRY WE LIVE IN, JAPAN, WILL BE EXEMPT FROM THAT?
THIS TALE TAKES PLACE IN JAPAN, AS THE CHAOTIC ENDING OF THE MILLENNIUM CLOSES IN.........

← EDITOR'S NOTE: PRETTY MUCH TRUE
IT'S A HEART-WARMING, COMEDIC HIGH SCHOOL ROMANCE WITH A TOUCH OF FANTASY FOR PEOPLE OF ALL AGES!!
SHIGURE ↓
TH-THAT SOUNDS LIKE IT COULD BE AMAZING OR A TOTAL LET-DOWN...
TOHRU ↓
← YUKI
IT'S GOT NOTHING TO DO WITH THE END OF THE WORLD.
KYO ↓

BONUS PREVIEW MANGA, PART 1

I'M SUPPOSED TO ANNOUNCE THE RETURN OF *FRUITS BASKET*...
...BUT I'VE GOT A BOMBSHELL TO DROP INSTEAD.
YUKI-KUN IS REALLY A...
...WOMAN!!
YUKI (RAT)
SHIGURE (DOG)
YOU KNOW, I THOUGHT MAYBE AN IMPACTFUL STATEMENT LIKE THAT WOULD BE A GOOD ATTENTION GRABBER.
I JUST WANTED... TO SAY SOMETHING LIKE THAT...
...OR SOMETHING...
TOHRU (MAIN CHARACTER)
KYO (CAT)
We'll be back soon! ♡

BONUS PREVIEW MANGA, PART 2

HEY, HANAJIMA, I USUALLY HATE GIRLY STUFF LIKE FORTUNE TELLIN'...
...BUT CAN YOU TELL ME IF I'M EVER GONNA BEAT YUKI?
...SURE.
FRUITS BASKET VOL. 1
NOW ON SALE!
DOKI (BA-DMP)
DOKI
GAN (GONG)
WHY ARE YOU TURNIN' AWAY FROM ME!?
......
SO... YOU'RE THE SUPERSTITIOUS TYPE, HUH?
I BET YOU CAN'T WHISTLE AT NIGHT.

THEY SAY IF YOU WHISTLE AT NIGHT...
...YOU'LL ATTRACT THIEVES!

BONUS PREVIEW MANGA, PART 3

SIDE STORY

SHIGURE-SAN, SHIGURE-SAN! OH MY GOSH!
I HEARD WE'RE GOING TO DO A DRAMA CD!!
AND NOT ONLY THAT, BUT IT'LL BE AN ORIGINAL STORY...
I WONDER WHAT'S GOING TO HAPPEN!?
HA-HA-HA! I KNOW EXACTLY WHAT IT'S ABOUT, TOHRU-KUN......
IT'LL HAVE...
...LOTS OF *cute, vivacious* HIGH SCHOOL GIRLS! IT'LL BE OVERFLOWING WITH *love*!
NOT EVEN CLOSE, SHIGURE-SAN.

LIKE I SAID, YOU'RE AN IDIOT.
I AIN'T AN IDIOT!
ON ONE FINE SUMMER'S DAY, THE CAST OF FRUITS BASKET...
NAGESHI SOUMEN!
...EMBARKS ON A PATH OF LOVE, COURAGE, AND NAGASHI SOUMEN.

BUT ALSO—FAILURE...
I'M SICK OF THIS.
WELL, THE STORY MAY OR MAY NOT BE LIKE THAT.
WHO CARES WHAT IT'S ABOUT?
THE IMPORTANT THING IS THAT WE APPEAR IN IT TOO!
HEY, AYAME, I'M TELLING YOU RIGHT NOW.
I'M NOT GOING TO BE IN IT.
ARE YOU LISTENING TO ME?
IN THE END... YOU'LL HAVE TO LISTEN FOR YOURSELF TO FIND OUT WHAT IT'S ABOUT...
WASABI
LAZINESS IS NOT AN ADMIRABLE QUALITY IN HUMANS...

THAT'S RIGHT!! I HAVE TO GET IT!!
THAT WAY I'LL BE ABLE TO HEAR KYO-KUN'S VOICE ANYTIME I WANT!!
TATTAKA (TMP)
たったか
TATTAKA
たったか
TATTAKA
たったか
I ALREADY MADE A RESERVATION AT A CD SHOP, BUT IS THAT THE BEST WAY TO GET A COPY!?
CD Shop Dodoitsu
アニメ
ゲーム
Mister! ♡ PLEASE GIVE ME THE FRUITS BASKET I RESERVED!!
CD Dodoitsu
HERE YOU GO!!
AND BECAUSE YOU'RE SO CUTE, I EVEN THREW IN A FEW BANANAS TOO!!
Yaaay! I'm so happy!!
CAUTION:
THE FRUITS BASKET SPECIAL CD SET IS NOT AVAILABLE IN BOOKSTORES, CD SHOPS, OR FRUIT STALLS.
PLEASE READ THE INSTRUCTIONS CAREFULLY IN ORDER TO OBTAIN THE CD.
EDITOR'S NOTE: THIS CD IS NO LONGER AVAILABLE AS OF SEPTEMBER 1999. IF YOUR FORM DID NOT REACH US BY THE DEADLINE, YOU WILL NOT RECEIVE A CD. THANK YOU FOR YOUR UNDERSTANDING.

RAIN SHELTER OF TERROR
ZAAA (SHHH)
SHEESH!
WHY'D IT HAVE TO START RAINING ALL OF A SUDDEN?
IT'S AN EVENING SHOWER, SO IF WE WAIT A BIT, IT'LL PASS OVER.
ZAAA
WHAT-EVER...
I JUST WANT IT TO STOP...
ZAAA
ZAAA
WHY ARE YOU CROUCHING DOWN THERE?
SCARED OF A LITTLE THUNDER?
WIMP!
LAME!
WUSS!
SHUT UP... OF COURSE I AIN'T SCARED...
KYO-KUN REALLY DOESN'T LIKE THE RAIN......
I LIKE THAT IT KEEPS HIM QUIET.
ZAAA
...I WISH THERE WAS SOME WAY TO GET HIS MIND OFF OF IT AT LEAST...
BUT...

LET'S TELL SCARY STORIES —!!!
AH HA HA HA HA
KNOW WHAT!? I READ A WHOLE BOOK OF INTERESTING SCARY STORIES!
THEY'RE SURE TO *THRILL YOU TO THE BONE* AND BEAT THE SUMMER HEAT!
HA!
EEEEK!!
YOU MEAN GRILL YOU TO THE BONE...
SHUT THE HELL UP, BOTH OF YOU!
YOU BOTH GOT IT WRONG!
SCARY STORIES SOUND GOOD TO ME.
IT'LL BE A GOOD WAY TO KILL TIME, WON'T IT?
NOT YOU TOO.
WHAT DO YOU THINK, YUKI...?
HUH...?
I DON'T MIND...
...BUT DON'T WE HAVE SOMEONE HERE WHO ISN'T A FAN OF THEM...?

HUH?
Oh, no, I'm fine with them, right?
Do...your worst?
IT DOESN'T LOOK LIKE SHE CAN HANDLE IT...
IF TOHRU DOESN'T WANT TO, THEN WE PROBABLY SHOULDN'T...
What!?
R-r-really, I don't mind...
HEY NOW, TOHRU.
YOU DON'T HAVE TO FORCE YOURSELF.
THAT'S RIGHT, TOHRU-KUN...
AS A MATTER OF FACT, I'M NOT PARTICULARLY FOND OF SCARY STORIES EITHER...
WHAT!!?

IS IT THAT SURPRISING ......?
WELL... UM...
DAMN STRAIGHT IT'S SURPRISING!!
HOW COULD YOU NOT LIKE SCARY STORIES!?
......
THE FACT THAT THEY CAN'T BE EXPLAINED...
...IS SO CREEPY......
ZAA (CHILLS)
AREN'T THEY CREEPY...?
BUT THOSE WORDS...
YOU'RE DESCRIBING YOURSELF, HANAJIMA!
I'D LIKE TO THROW THOSE WORDS BACK IN HER FACE!!
SHE'S KEEPING AT IT...!!

ARE YOU TWO OKAY?
AH, Y-YES!!
I-I JUST DON'T LIKE THE PART WHEN SCARY STORIES START GETTING SCARY...
I'M FINE IF THEY'RE NOT SCARY, BUT FOR SOME REASON, ALL THE ONES I'VE HEARD ARE SCARY...
HEY. AIN'T THAT THE WHOLE POINT OF "SCARY STORIES"?
IF YOU IGNORE THE STORY AND THINK OF A COMEDY ROUTINE INSTEAD, YOU PROBABLY WON'T GET SCARED...
I SEE WHERE YOU'RE COMING FROM, BUT WHY FORCE HERSELF TO LISTEN IN THE FIRST PLACE AT THAT POINT?
OH! THAT'S IT!
I KNOW WHAT YOU CAN DO!
Just cover your ears!!
わっし
WASSHI (FWAP)
AGAIN, WHY WOULD WE GO THAT FAR WHEN WE CAN JUST...NOT?

THERE WE GO! SO LET'S START, LET'S START!
IT HAPPENED ONE HUMID AFTERNOON ON A LATE SUMMER'S DAY...
WHAT, YOU'RE STARTING ALREADY!?
HE WAS WAITING FOR THIS, WASN'T HE...?
REMEMBERING HOW THIRSTY HE WAS, A BOY HEADED FOR THE KITCHEN...
MIIN (BUZZ)
MIIN
MIIN
THERE HE FOUND A GLASS OF ICED COFFEE LOOKING FRESHLY POURED, JUST SITTING OUT ON THE COUNTER......
THINKING IT WAS A GODSEND, HE DRANK IT DOWN...
GOKU (GULP)
GOKU
GOKU
GOKU
BUT IN THE NEXT MOMENT, A CHILL RAN DOWN HIS SPINE.
HE REALIZED THE TERRIBLE ACTION HE HAD JUST TAKEN.
HE STARED...
...AT THE EMPTY GLASS.
HE WAS UNABLE TO AVERT HIS EYES OR EVEN MOVE A MUSCLE.
FOR NESTLED IN THAT GLASS...

...WAS A SINGLE BLACK COCKROACH...!
WHOA, THAT WAS SCARY!! TOTALLY SCARY, MAN!!
!?
FREAKIN' GROSS!! ....
THE SEQUEL INVOLVES GRATED CHEESE...
WE DON'T WANNA HEAR ANY MORE!

W-W-WAS IT REALLY THAT SCARY......!?
NO... IT WAS NO BIG DEAL...
WHAT !?
WERE YOU SCARED?
I'M GONNA HURL!
IT WASN'T SCARY, JUST DISGUSTING!! WHAT BOOK DID HE GET THAT OUT OF!!?
WAIT, YOU WERE LISTENIN' THE WHOLE TIME!!?
SHIGURE ......
HOW MANY PEN NAMES DO YOU HAVE...?
SO IT WAS YOU...YOU'RE TO BLAME...
YES? WHAT'S UP?
JACKASS... HOW MANY MORE DISGUSTING BOOKS DO YOU GOT LEFT IN YOU...?

TIME TO RESTART!

YEAR OF THE RABBIT
CELEBRATE!

I apologize for the wait and thank you for being so patient. From here on out, there may be times when I make you nervous again, but please continue to support me. I will do my very best.

CELEBRATING ♥ THE REVIVAL OF *FURUBA*! GREETINGS PAGE

LONG TIME NO SEE!
I'M TOHRU HONDA, AND WE'RE FINALLY BACK!
PLEASE CONTINUE TO SUPPORT US!!
?
TOHRU-KUN, TOHRU-KUN! I JUST HAD A GREAT IDEA!
SINCE WE'VE BEEN ON HIATUS FOR SO LONG, DON'T YOU GET THE FEELING WE COULD CHANGE THE STORY AND NOBODY WOULD NOTICE THE DIFFERENCE!? MAYBE SOMETHING LIKE ***"HEART-THROBBING ☆ TALE OF MOVING IN TOGETHER"*** STARRING JUST YOU AND ME! WHAT DO YOU SAY, SHALL WE CHANGE IT!? SHALL WE CHANGE IT!?
SHALL WE CHANGE IT!?
WHA ...?
NO CHANGING IT.

I apologize for keeping you waiting for so long! After a one-year absence, Tohru and friends are back!! Please give me your support. ♥

• Contents Details 2 •

After Chapter 44, published in Issue 18, 2000 of *Hana to Yume*, Takaya-sensei took an approximately one-year hiatus due to medical treatment. Then, in the summer of 2001, the magazine announced the series was resuming at long last.

♥ Rain Shelter of Terror ♥

Published in 2001 in *Fruits Basket Special*, a special issue of *Hana to Yume*
(Included in *Hana to Yume Comics*, Volume 9)

A *Furuba* side story, the first one in a long time, for the special issue. It also included info on the TV anime, which began its run in May 2001. Everyone was so excited!

♥ Time to Restart! ♥

Published in 2001 in *Fruits Basket Special*, a special issue of *Hana to Yume*, and in Issue 18, 2001 of *Hana to Yume*

An announcement that the series was resuming, which ran in the *Fruits Basket Special* issue and *Hana to Yume* magazine proper. ♪

♥ Celebrating ♥ the Revival of *Furuba*! Greetings Page ♥

Published in Issue 19, 2001 of *Hana to Yume*

This issue didn't just resume the series—it also had a color opening page for Chapter 45 and this greetings page included with the main story.

♥ Bonus Drama CD Side Story ♥

Published in the 2/1 Issue, 2005 of *The Hana to Yume*

A side story that introduced the *Sparkling Wonderful ★ CD*, included in Issue 4, 2005.

I'M YUKI SOHMA, A FIRST-YEAR HIGH SCHOOL STUDENT. I WAS BORN IN THE YEAR OF THE DOG.
ALTHOUGH I'M THE RAT...
I'M KYO SOHMA, FIRST-YEAR HIGH SCHOOL STUDENT, YEAR OF THE BOAR......
...I'M THE CAT...
I'M TOHRU HONDA. I'M A FIRST-YEAR HIGH SCHOOL STUDENT, AND I WAS BORN IN THE YEAR OF THE CAT!
JUST KIDDING! WHAT DO YOU THINK MY ZODIAC ANIMAL REALLY IS?
I'LL GIVE YOU TIME TO THINK!

Published in the bonus *Quiz Book*, which came with Issue 18, 1998 of *Hana to Yume*

★The answer is on page 224!

Bonus Drama CD Side Story

THIS DRAMA CD CONSISTS OF A CONVERSATION AMONG THE STUDENT COUNCIL MEMBERS. THE CONTENTS ARE BOTH HEARTWARMING AND BEAUTIFUL. THIS ITEM IS A TEARJERKER THAT IS OVERFLOWING WITH NATURAL LOVE. BELOW IS A SHORT, EXCLUSIVE SNEAK PEEK OF THE BONUS.

NAO-CHAN, YOU'RE REALLY ANNOYING ME.
CUT IT OUT AL-READY.
IT'S NOT LIKE I WANT TO GRIPE! YOU'RE ALL JUST SO IDIOTIC!
I'M NOT...
...NOT ANGRY.
KIMI BROKE UP BEFORE COMING HERE, YOU KNOW?
I'LL HIRE A SPECIAL SCIENTIFIC INVESTIGATION UNIT TO DISCOVER THE TRUTH!!
YOU BROKE UP.

THAT SNEAK PEEK JUMPS AROUND TOO MUCH! I HAVE NO IDEA WHAT THE STORY'S ABOUT!!!
A REAL TEAR-JERKER...
NO, MAN, THAT TOTALLY MADE ME TEAR UP!
I'M SUPPOSED TO SAY THAT!?
IT'S OBVIOUSLY NOT A TEAR-JERKER!!!
But isn't it...a story that'll tug on your heart-strings...? Right...?
WEREN'T YOU SAYING SOMETHING ABOUT A BREAK UP...?
HERE, SAKURAGI-KUN...
DRIED SARDINES.
FROM THE PRESIDENT... AND ME.
ワンダフルにぼし
ファミリーパック
WHAT'S THAT GOT TO DO WITH ANY-THING!?
THERE, THERE! IT'S FINE!
GUORI (GRIND)
GO
AAARRGUGH!
JUST! EAT! THEM!
GORI
GORI
GORI
DELISH!
AH HA HA
PLEASE LISTEN TO THE CD TO FIND OUT IF ANY OF THE ABOVE IS ACCURATE.
PACKAGE: WONDERFUL SARDINES / FAMILY PACK

SOHMA FAMILY DIARY

SHIGURE-SAN: "I CAN'T STAND THAT, SO PLEASE STOP."

THE WRAPPING PAPER ON THIS YEAR-END GIFT THAT CAME FOR SHIGURE-SAN...IT'S REALLY PRETTY.
IT WOULD BE A WASTE TO THROW AWAY THIS STRING TOO... MAYBE I CAN USE IT FOR SOME-THING...?
...
IT DOESN'T LOOK HALF BAD AS A RIBBON...
I'LL WEAR IT IN MY HAIR TO SCHOOL TOMORROW...
I WAS RIGHT!
I'LL BUY YOU ONE ......!!
びくぅっ
BIKUU (JUMP)
HUH!?
I'LL BUY YOU ONE, SO PLEASE—DON'T DO THIS TO ME...!!

BLOOD WILL TELL
EVERY TIME AAYA AND MINE GO OUT...
...HE PUTS ON HER SHOES FOR HER...
IT'S JUST SO STRANGE, ISN'T IT!!?
SIGN: AYAME: TRUST IS NUMBER ONE, TREASURING THE HEART
信用第一
あや
AND THEY'RE ALWAYS LIKE THAT! ALWAYS!!
I FEEL EMBARRASSED JUST LOOKING AT THEM!!
REGULAR CUSTOMERS
ONE'S AS BAD AS THE OTHER!! THEY'RE FOOLS IN LOVE!
SINCE YOU'RE HERE VISITING, YOU SHOULD LET THEM KNOW TO TONE IT DOWN ALREADY!
HA HA...
BUT IS IT REALLY SO STRANGE...?
IF I'M BEING HONEST, I CAN... KIND OF SEE THE APPEAL THERE...
WHAT'S WRONG? DID SOMETHING JUST SHAKE THE FOUNDATIONS OF YOUR WORLD!?
MY LITTLE BROTHER!

"TAKE THAT," YOU SAY?

KYO-KUN...? WHAT ARE OTOU-SAMA'S HOBBIES...?
WHAT DOES HE LIKE...?
GRRR!
THIS GIRL...SHE DOESN'T KNOW WHEN TO GIVE UP...!
MASTER HATES WOMEN WHO DRESS IN BLACK MOST OF ALL!!
TAKE THAT!!
I'LL DO ANYTHING TO KEEP THEM APART!! EVEN LIE!!
TOO BAD FOR YOU, HANAJIMA...
TOO BAD...?
GYU (CLENCH)
OH MY. IS THAT RIGHT...?
HEE HEE...
YOU THINK THAT DON'T APPLY TO YOU!?
YOU!! I'M TALKIN' ABOUT YOU!!
WHERE'S THAT CONFIDENT GRIN COMIN' FROM!?

IS IT OKAY TO DRAW HIM SO HAPPY?
(CONSIDERING THE SITUATION IN THE MAIN STORY...)
IN CHAPTER 74...
HE'S THE KIND OF GUY WHO WOULDN'T BE BOTHERED EVEN IF HE STEPPED IN A STEAMING PILE OF DOG CRAP...
...IS HOW UO-CHAN APPRAISED KURENO-SAN.
BUT HOW WOULD HE REACT IF THAT REALLY HAPPENED TO HIM?
KURENO-SAN, YOU STEPPED ON A TURD!
AHHH!
OH...?
HA-HA!
SO I DID. I DIDN'T EVEN NOTICE.
I'D BETTER PAY MORE ATTENTION, RIGHT?
......
I LOVE THIS BASTARD!!
ZUGYUUUN (THUNK)
OH, WELL, IT LOOKS LIKE ALL WOULD BE FINE, HUH?

NO ROOM FOR A QUIET PERSON TO INTERJECT

GURE-SAN, DO YOU KNOW WHY TORI-SAN OF ALL PEOPLE CAN'T PARTICIPATE IN THE DRAMA CD!?
"BECAUSE HE WON'T TALK!" CAN YOU BELIEVE THAT!? WHAT IS THIS WORLD COMING TO!?
AAYA, YOU TALK SO MUCH THAT HE CAN'T GET A WORD IN. THAT'S WHY HE CAN'T BE IN IT.
SO I THOUGHT TO MY-SELF!!
BOOK: MOMOTARO
IF HE WON'T TALK, THEN I'LL JUST FORCE HIM TO TALK!!
I'LL MAKE HIM READ A STORY!!
ももたろう
ずばん
ZUBAN (SWISH)
HOW-EVER!!
TORI-SAN DOESN'T USUALLY TALK MUCH, SO IF THAT BEAUTIFUL VOICE OF HIS WERE TO BECOME HOARSE FROM READING THIS LONG STORY, IT WOULD BE A SERIOUS AFFAIR FOR THE SOHMA FAMILY!!
THEREFORE, I SHALL NOBLY FILL IN FOR TORI-SAN!!
LONG, LONG AGO AND FAR AWAY, THERE WAS AN OLD COUPLE WHO WAS IN FOR A SURPRISE!!
READ QUIETER.
BUT WHY A FAIRY TALE?
ROGER THAT, TORI-SAN!!

ALL YOU NEED IS LOVE

RICCHAN AND MICCHAN...
...ARE ON ANOTHER DATE TODAY.
THE WIND IS A LITTLE CHILLY TODAY, ISN'T IT?
AH!
YES...IT IS CERTAINLY CHILLY SPRING WEATHER. MITSURU-SAN, WOULD YOU LIKE TO PUT ON THIS SHAWL...?
I WORE ANOTHER LONG-SLEEVED KIMONO AGAIN WITHOUT EVEN THINKING ABOUT IT...!!
I'M SO LUCKY...
LUCKY THAT MITSURU-SAN IS A WOMAN WHO ISN'T BOTHERED BY MINOR SCREW-UPS...
WHY DOES HE ALWAYS WEAR KIMONOS ON OUR DATES...?
I CAN'T JUST ASK HIM, "WAIT, ARE YOU ACTUALLY A WOMAN?" I MEAN, I'M PRETTY SURE HE'S A MAN, BUT COULD IT BE...? NO, NO. WHAT AM I THINKING...?
OH...
LOOK! THE CHERRY BLOSSOMS OVER THERE ARE IN BLOOM...
OH YES... SHALL WE HEAD THAT WAY?
WELL, THEY SEEM HAPPY.

AND YET, THEY'RE ALL AT THE TOP OF THEIR CLASS

THESE NUMBERS ARE OFF...
IT SEEMS LIKE YOU'VE BEEN GETTING ALONG WITH MACHI LATELY, BUT DON'T BE A TWO-TIMER, YUN-YUN.
I'M NOT A TWO-TIMER!
MM-HMM, SURE. AS A BIG BROTHER, I JUST CAN'T LOOK THE OTHER WAY HERE.
WHY DOES THIS GUY ONLY ACT LIKE HER BIG BROTHER WHEN IT COMES TO STUPID CRAP...?
DON'T YOU HAVE ANYTHING BETTER TO DO?
BISHI (POINT)
MACHI...
IF YOU'RE A MAN, YOU SHOULD COME RIGHT OUT WITH IT. YOU MUST CHOOSE!
ZUBISHI (JERK)
...OR ME!!?
YOU!!?
HE CHOOSES KIMI!
RIGHT, YUN-YUN?
SHUT UP AND GET BACK TO WORK!!!

WHAT IF KYO READ VOLUME 17 (PARTICULARLY CHAPTERS 97 AND 98)?
WHAT ARE THE HIGHLIGHTS OF FURUBA, VOLUME 17, AGAIN?
MAYBE WHAT'S GOING ON WITH AKITO-SAN...
KII (SCREECH)
COW-TITS!!
NO. TITS!!
THE SORDID, MELO-DRAMATIC MOTHER-DAUGHTER FIGHT WITH REN-SAN?
HATORI-SAN, WHO GETS CAUGHT BETWEEN THEM AND LOOKS LIKE HE'S GOING TO COLLAPSE FROM ANXIETY?
NO... UH, I WAS FINE...
THEN THERE'S SHIGURE-SAN, WHO PAYS NO ATTENTION TO ANY OF THAT AS HE LIVES HIS SELF-CENTERED LIFE?
THAT'S NOT TRUE! I DO THINK ABOUT THE PEOPLE AROUND ME.
YOU'VE GOT ME ALL WRONG!
OR MAYBE...
WHY...?
HE SEEMED LIKE SUCH A QUIET GUY!! IS HE TRYIN' TO COP A FEEL!?
IF ALL HE'S DOIN' IS EXPLAINING THE SITUATION TO HER, THERE'S NO NEED TO GET ALL TOUCHY-FEELY!! STOP TOUCHING TOHRU!! KURENO!!
AH!
KYO-KUN, IS THERE ANYTHING SPECIAL YOU'D LIKE FOR DINNER!?
DEEP-FRIED CHICKEN...!
Furuba
Furuba 17

Special Character-Contest-General-Comments Manga (!?), **Sohma Family Festival**

NICE TO MEET YOU AND HELLO. I'M TAKAYA.
THANK YOU FOR BUYING THIS FAN BOOK.
THANK YOU!
STAND-IN: MOGETA
TO COMMEMORATE... I DON'T KNOW IF THAT'S THE RIGHT WORD, BUT NOW THAT WE'VE REACHED THE END, I'D LIKE TO TALK A LITTLE BIT ABOUT *FURUBA*.
DUE TO LIMITED SPACE, I CAN'T TALK ABOUT ALL THE CHARACTERS, SO I HOPE YOU UNDERSTAND.
ALL RIGHT.
WE HELD OUR FINAL CHARACTER POPULARITY CONTEST.
THANK YOU FOR VOTING!
KYO-KUN WON BY A LANDSLIDE IN ALL THE CONTESTS, FIRST PLACE EVERY TIME. I GUESS HE'S POPULAR?
I WONDER WHY...
HEY......
WHAT DO YOU MEAN, "YOU WONDER"!?
I THINK I KNOW...

IT'S BECAUSE KYO-KUN IS SO KIND AND HANDSOME, YET BASHFUL AT TIMES—
MMPH!
YOU DON'T GOTTA GO ON AND ON ABOUT ME...
THAT'S ENOUGH OUTTA YOU...
I'M GRATEFUL EVERYONE IS FOND OF HIM.
SUCH LOVE...
I'M GRATEFUL THAT EVERYONE LIKES TOHRU TOO.
I REALLY PUT HER THROUGH THE WRINGER...
...BUT IF SHE WEREN'T THE MAIN CHARACTER, I COULDN'T HAVE MADE *FURUBA*.
SO I'M THANKFUL I CREATED TOHRU.
I'M THANKFUL!
HEY...
AREN'T YOU A LITTLE COLD TO ME, COMPARED TO HOW YOU TREAT HER?
GIMME A BREAK...
NAH, YOU'VE GOT IT WRONG. IF I WAS REALLY COLD TO YOU, I WOULDN'T HAVE LET YOU GET TOGETHER WITH TOHRU.
WHAT!!?
YOU DON'T PULL YOUR PUNCHES, DO YOU...!?
SHE SAID IT...

WELL, LOOK—DIDN'T TEASING KYO-KUN HELP MAKE HIM WHO HE IS NOW?
AH!
I SEE WHAT YOU MEAN.
YUKI REALLY GREW DURING THE SERIES, DIDN'T HE?
IT'S LIKE YUKI'S FEELINGS NEAR THE END......
I CAN SAY THIS NOW THAT IT'S OVER.
WHEN I FIRST CREATED YUKI, I ENVISIONED HIM AS *FURUBA'S* OTHER MAIN CHARACTER.
IT WAS SUPPOSED TO BE LIKE A RECORD OF HIS GROWTH.
COME TO THINK OF IT... AFTER YUKI SHARED HIS FEELINGS WITH KAKERU...
...HE CHANGED THE KIND OF CLOTHES HE WORE AND TRIMMED HIS ONCE-LONG NAILS.
DID YOU NOTICE THOSE CHANGES...?
THEY'RE TOO MINOR TO NOTICE.
AND AFTER KYO HEARD THE TALE OF "THE FOOLISH TRAVELER," HE STOPPED CALLING TOHRU AN IDIOT.
DID YOU NOTICE ...?
NOBODY NOTICED.
YOU CARE TOO MUCH ABOUT LITTLE DETAILS LIKE THAT!
AWW ...

WHY AM I THE ONLY ONE WHO'S COSPLAYING?
AKITO GREW TOO, DIDN'T SHE?
IF SHE REALLY WERE A MAN...
...I WOULD'VE BEEN TEMPTED TO HAVE THEM GET TOGETHER. IT'S FUN TO THINK ABOUT NOW, ISN'T IT...?
YOU JUST OPENED UP A CAN OF WORMS.
ぎしぎし
GISHI (PULL)
GISHI
ぎし
GISHI
HEEEEY!!!
WHAT'D YOU JUST SAY!?
NOW THAT I THINK ABOUT IT...
...ARE YOU SURE YOU'RE REALLY HAPPY WITH SHIGURE, AKKI?
SOMETIMES I FEEL A BIT BA—
OKAY, NOW YOU'VE CROSSED THE LINE. ♡
GOT IT.

AS FOR SHIGURE-SAN, WHO STAYED ON HIS OWN PATH TO THE VERY END (TO THE POINT WHERE HE FELT OUT OF PLACE IN *FURUBA*)...
...I WANT HIM TO TAKE GOOD CARE OF AKITO-SAN.
I WILL, I WILL!
WHEN THE SERIES BEGAN...
...SOMEONE ASKED ME WHO WAS STRONGER, AKITO OR HANA-CHAN?
OH, THAT'S RIGHT!
OF COURSE...
...IT'S HANA-CHAN.
HANA-CHAN IS ON MEMO DISTRIBUTION DUTY
BOOK: MEMOS
IN FACT, SHE'S THE STRONGEST CHARACTER IN *FURUBA*.
SHE'S THE "SECRET BOSS."
SECRET BOSSES ARE SO TOUGH THESE DAYS, IT'S NOT EVEN FUNNY...
ZUGAAAN (WHAM)
DODOOON (BAM)
I HAD FUN DRAWING HER TOGETHER WITH MEGUMI.
I HOPE THINGS GO WELL FOR HER AND MASTER...
ACTUALLY, I ENJOYED DRAWING ALL THE FEMALE CHARACTERS.
ALTHOUGH IT WAS DIFFICULT...
OUT OF EVERY-ONE...

...I LIKED DRAWING KISA BEST.
SO MUCH SO THAT I'LL GIVE HER A CLOSE-UP FOR NO REASON...
I BET SHE'LL BE A BEAUTY WHEN SHE GROWS UP!
RIGHT?
YEAH.
A REAL BEAUTY.
I HAVE THE FEELING MOMIJI WILL GET EVEN TALLER AND MORE MASCULINE.
NOT A HOST
KIND AS HE IS, I'M SURE HE'LL BE POPULAR WITH THE LADIES!
MOMICCHI AND TOHRU GETTING TOGETHER WAS ANOTHER OPTION I CONSIDERED...
I TOLD YOU...
ENOUGH OF THAT CRAP!
ぎりぎり
GIRI (TWIST)
GIRI
ぎりぎり
GIRI
GIRI
SHUT UP! I DON'T WANNA HEAR ANY MORE! I WON'T ACCEPT THIS...
I GET THE FEELING I COULD'VE PUT TOHRU WITH ANYONE, AND THEY WOULD HAVE MADE A NATURAL COUPLE......
YOU JUST CAN'T HELP YOURSELF, HUH...?

UM...
BUT, UM, THE ONLY ONE FOR ME...
...IS KYO-KUN...
YOU'RE RIGHT. AT THE END OF THE DAY, KYO-KUN REALLY IS THE BEST MATCH FOR TOHRU-KUN.
THEY DID GET VOTED NUMBER ONE FOR "BEST COUPLE" AFTER ALL.
YOU'RE RUNNING OUT OF PAGES, BY THE WAY.
OH, SORRY. I HAD MORE TO SAY, BUT I GUESS I BETTER WRAP IT UP.
THANK YOU SO MUCH FOR READING *FRUITS BASKET*.
THIS STORY IS OVER, BUT TOHRU-KUN IS LEADING A HAPPY LIFE EVEN NOW.
PLEASE REVISIT TOHRU AND THE OTHERS IN THESE BOOKS ANYTIME YOU LIKE.
PLEASE DO!
THANKS SO MUCH!
COME ON, YOU SAY GOODBYE TOO!
DON'T SULK!
HOW CAN YOU COMPLAIN? YOU GOT VOTED "NUMBER ONE BEST COUPLE"!
......

ちゅっ
CHU (KISS)
!!
HOW DO YOU LIKE THEM APPLES !!!?
YEAH, YEAH, YOU WIN.
BUT WHAT ARE YOU TRYING TO PROVE?
DON'T DO IT AND THEN GET ALL BASHFUL. YOU'RE MAKING ME EMBARRASSED.
THE END

For the 900th Issue of Hana to Yume

Congratulatory Four-Panel Manga

CONGRATULATIONS ON THE 900TH ISSUE OF *HANA TO YUME!*
NOT THAT IT'S MY PLACE, BUT I WOULD LIKE TO CELEBRATE ...
I'M KIND OF NERVOUS ...
... YEAH, WELL.
IT FEELS LIKE COMING HOME AFTER A LONG ABSENCE, DOESN'T IT?
WHY DON'T WE HAVE EVERYONE LOSE THEIR MEMORIES ...
...AND START THE STORY OVER FROM SCRATCH!?
UUUM...
IS THAT WHAT THE GUY WHO'S LIVED HIS WHOLE LIFE ON HIS OWN TERMS SAYS...?
YOU DON'T CARE HOW DIFFICULT IT WAS TO GET OUR HAPPY ENDINGS THE FIRST TIME, HUH...?
I'M SORRY. *I'M REALLY SORRY.*

Contents Details 3

Two fan books, *Cat* and *Banquet*, were published in 2005 and 2007 respectively. Each of them contained eight pages of new material drawn especially for the occasion.

♥ Sohma Family Diary ♥

2005
Published in *Fruits Basket Fan Book (Cat)*

A side story created especially for the first official fan book.

♥ Sohma Family Festival ♥

2007
Published in *Fruits Basket Fan Book (Banquet)*

The second official fan book contained a side story created especially for the book. That same volume also contained the results of the character contests, republished in this volume on pages 244–245.

Congratulatory Four-Panel Manga for ♥ the 900th Issue of *Hana to Yume* ♥

Published in Issue 15, 2010 of *Hana to Yume*

Even after the series was over, *Furuba* participated in *Hana to Yume*'s precious celebratory party! ♪

I'M YEAR OF THE DOG!
WOOF-WOOF!

Published in the bonus *Quiz Book*, which came with Issue 18, 1998 of *Hana to Yume*

MEMORIAL FILE

※Note: Some of these were taken from articles in the two official fan books (*Cat* and *Banquet*), expanded with new material, and reedited.

Twitter
#iloveFuruba

Tell Us Your Favorite Line from *Furuba*!

RESULTS

Popularity Contest
No.1
38 votes

The most important thing is the desire to overcome our weaknesses.

—Yuki Sohma
Chapter 28

COMMENT

@ruu_48: That really hit home. I have my own issues, and I've thought, "Why am I this weak? I hate myself like this." I beat myself up, but it's okay to be weak. You can stand up against it. His line gave me courage. Thank you very much, Yuki.

Other Opinions
@otyaumai100: I was in middle school, but I stopped going. But then I wrote this line on my student notebook and started going again. It's a good memory.
@omusubi0615: I love tons of lines in *Furuba*, but this one in particular encouraged me back then.
@pickalice: This gives you courage to take the first step.
@7p0p5: This is my creed. Delicate weakness over cold strength. *Furuba* taught me that weakness may actually be kindness.
@kanoa0823: Seeing Kisa move forward made me realize that I needed to change too. How will I stand and walk forward from a point of weakness? If I fall, how will I rise? I want to do my best, like Kisa.
@yoppyclara: This line always comes back to me when I'm in a hopeless situation.
@secondmoon2: I've gotten courage many times from reading *Furuba*, but I think this line is the most potent. When the going gets tough and sticking it out doesn't do the trick, I've often chanted this line to myself!
@mepotyaro: I always remember this when I'm scared. I feel like I've gotten a little stronger after reading this line.
@sakurako2140: I've gotten courage many times from this line!

It's not like...I've suddenly gotten any stronger. And nothing has changed. I'm still trembling. But...let's still face our fears.
The most important thing is the desire to overcome our weaknesses.

Also from that Scene

@fcle_iy: I always think of this line when I want to change.
@_2884948295243: "The most important thing is the desire to overcome our weaknesses" has become my mantra.
@lvkjkfskh: This line has helped me time and time again...When it looked like I was going to fail, I remembered Yuki-kun's words and was able to do my best.
@keneko: Back when I was feeling self-hatred and had lost sight of myself, this line taught me that even if I didn't know what my goal was, I couldn't let my spirit die. Even now, as an adult, this line supports me.

Popularity Contest
No.2
22 votes

But...as for me, I want to live with the burden of memories. Even the sad memories... Even the memories that hurt me...Even the memories I wish I could forget. I have faith that if I keep doing my best to bear that burden without running away, I'll eventually become strong enough that memories like that won't get me down. I want to believe that. I want to believe that not a single memory should be forgotten.

—Momiji Sohma
Chapter 23

COMMENT

@1mtAct: I'm moved every time I read this line!! Even with tough memories, reading this line helps me overcome them!! Natsuki Takaya-sensei! Thank you for creating *Furuba*!!

Other Opinions
@velizu: I really like Momiji-kun's line in Volume 4. No matter how many times I read the manga or watch the anime, tears come to my eyes at this line about treasuring even the painful memories.
@hanahanasyobu: Momiji's line in Volume 4 has stuck with me ever since I was a kid. Even if there's something painful in your life, try to become a person who can overcome it "until they become precious memories..." Many lines have saved me, but these words have made the biggest impression on me.
@sakura801cat: Many lines from *Furuba* have resonated with me, and I love them all! Words that I especially treasure even now are from Momiji, who said something like, "There are no memories that it's okay to forget."

Also from that Scene

That's why I really didn't want Mama to forget me. I didn't want her to give up. But this is just me being selfish. This is all between you and me.

@killrack: I'm going with a scene over a line. It's in Chapter 23, where we see Momicchi's sweet strength that ends with "This is all between you and me."
@kazutan_224: I love Momiji's line in Volume 4!! It's a scene that makes me think maybe Momiji is the most mature of them all.

Popularity Contest
No.3
15 votes

...Maybe you should start by washing the laundry at your feet first.
It is important to think about what lies ahead, but if you only focus on that, you'll trip over the laundry at your feet, right?
So it's also important to think about what you can do right now, today.
If you do that, washing one piece of laundry at a time—before you know it, the sun will be out, beaming down on you.
And sure, you'll still feel anxiety from time to time, but when that happens, take a little break.

—Shigure Sohma
Chapter 46

COMMENT

@Aki_s67: When things are stressed and I'm nervous, remembering these words lets me take a step back and calm down. Right now, it's my favorite motto. (LOL)

Other Opinions

@mncsm: I love Shigure-san's laundry speech. Right now, I'm thinking about changing jobs, but there are so many things I have to do that I don't know where to start. Keeping Shigure-san and Tohru-kun's conversation in mind, I'm going to start with what's in front of me! That's what I keep saying to myself.
@xxxsayurinxxx: For years now, every time I've been swamped, I think about Shigure-san's line here.
@rippi_mayo: These words have supported me ever since elementary school. Even so, there are times when I overthink things, but if I become anxious because of that, these words quickly pop into my head. Thank you, Shigure-san. Thank you, Takaya-sensei.
@minaki_sakaki: I love the laundry speech. At the time, I was in a conundrum about what to do after high school, so I remember how those lines really resonated with me.
@nonoko_nl: Gure-san is a scumbag, but I love the side of him that dispenses advice on life like this. (That's a compliment.)
@Enda3139: When I was anxious about my future, this line really gave me emotional support. ;_;
@twinklesmile38: I always worry about the future, so these words hit home the hardest. *Furuba* is my bible!!
@show9ko300: I remember this line every time I can't move from being anxious and overthinking things. You have to wash the laundry at your feet first, one piece at a time.

Your teacher advises you to "like yourself."
What does that even mean? "Good points," it says...
How is one supposed to find those...?
I only know things that I hate about myself.
And because that's all I know, I hate myself more.
So...forcing myself to look for my good points is a stretch.
It's an empty exercise......
That advice is off the mark. Your teacher has it backward.
I don't think you can like yourself...
until someone says that they like you first.
When someone accepts you, you can start accepting yourself.
I think that's when...liking yourself becomes possible......

—Yuki Sohma
Chapter 28

COMMENT

@jagapote10: "I don't think you can like yourself until someone says that they like you first"...This has stuck with me the most. There was a time when I was so afraid of being left out that I would feel anxious about doing anything alone. I felt like I would be hated for being alone. Maybe that's why I remember this. It sometimes comes to mind, even today.

Other Opinions
@cmaqll: The lines before and after these lines really get me too. Trust in Yuki-kun.
@nako244: I can't count how many lines I love from *Furuba*, but if I had to choose just one, it's Yuki-kun's words to Kisa: "I don't think you can like yourself until someone says that they like you first." *Furuba* has always been the bible of my heart!!
@yuwa_05: Yuki talking to Kisa about going to school. Those are the first lines that came to mind when I read "favorite line." Even when I remember those words now, their warmth soothes any wound.

Every so often,
we'll still think of you.
"Is she doing well?"
"She's not crying, is she?"
"Is she smiling even now?
"Is she happy today too?"
That's how we think of you.
It's how we'll always
think of you.

—Yuki Sohma
The Final Chapter

COMMENT

@love_tearsxxx: I remember crying hysterically when I read this.

Also from that Scene

Thank you...
I'm so glad
I met you...I'm...
so glad you were here.
Thank you...Thank you.
...Thank you...Tohru.

@chiiimosh: There are other lines that give me courage on a personal level when I read them, but Yuki's words here made me feel, "Ahhh, *Furuba* really is over!" I cry every time I read those words. To be honest, there are so many wonderful lines in *Furuba* it's hard to choose!
@soukyu24: As you'd expect from the ending, I cried like a baby. I have to say thank you too.
@hiiragiiwashi: *Furuba* has so much precious dialogue and so many beloved scenes there's no way I can choose just one favorite, but of them all, these lines are special. The emotions from twenty-three volumes are condensed into these words......
@chanzuvivi: In all of *Furuba*, Yuki has grown the most as a character. I think these lines are his and *Furuba*'s culmination, so they made me cry the most. This was such a great scene.

Father...
I don't want to be "special"
or a "god" anymore.
Is it okay for me to be...
just myself...?
I can start...living my
own life?
......
I..."I" will be miserable...
and afraid...
and unneeded...
but still...

—Akito Sohma
Chapter 130

COMMENT

@hiiragiiti: I felt so sorry for Akito. After losing everything that was precious to her one by one, she cried, accepting it.

Other Opinions
@natuxnatux115: A long time ago, I loved Kyo-kun, but as an adult, and after rereading the series as an adult, Akito-san chokes me up with emotion. She's cowardly and weak, but I like how straightforward and pure she is.
@rin0210a: I've always loved Akito-san.
@yuyu_siki_A: She's precious, saying those lines a couple of words at a time through her tears. Akito-san becoming more feminine near the end made a huge impression on me.
@hi_sanachan: While reading, I prayed for her happiness. I really love her.

Maybe it's stuck on your back... If a person's greatest quality is like a pickled plum in a rice ball... that "plum" might be stuck on the back side. All over the world, on everyone's backs, are pickled plums of various forms, colors, and flavors...but because each one is on a person's back, those tasty plums may go unnoticed. "I have nothing. I'm just plain white rice." Even though it isn't true... Even though everyone has a fine pickled plum on their back... Maybe people get jealous because they can clearly see the plums on others' backs.

—Tohru Honda
Chapter 8

COMMENT

@camellia2006: This left a very deep impression. I thought it was a wonderful way of looking at things.

Other Opinions
@_chilamp: I was still young the first time I read this, so I didn't really understand the meaning then, but after reading it again some years later, I was like, "I-I see!" And I agreed with the sentiment.
@knry051: I love Tohru-kun's talk about the pickled plum on a rice ball! It's true—we do often notice other people's good points instead of our own.

Also from that Scene

Even now, someone might be envious of another. They may be longing for something without realizing that they already have it. Thinking of it that way makes me want to...work just a little harder as I am now.

@colar88call: This has saved me time and time again...
@_ice__biscuit: I love this chapter's pickled plum analogy! (･ω･)♡

There's also a feeling you won't get unless you hit rock bottom. You rebel against the ideals in life...but then everything goes bad, and for the first time, you find yourself yearning for those ideals. Pain would mean nothing without kindness. Darkness can't stand out without the sun. Neither is something to scoff at. Both sides of the equation have meaning. So even if you stumble and make mistakes, it isn't for nothing. If you think to yourself, "I won't let this be for nothing!" it'll turn into something that will help you grow. That's...the way I see it.

—Kyoko Honda
Chapter 41

COMMENT

@nappa_CFlove318: Kyoko-san's words here give me strength.

Another Opinion
@knry051: I get depressed easily, so Kyoko-san's lines really resonated with me.

Let's walk together...
hand in hand.
Through the joyous times...
and the sad...
The cycle repeating itself,
again and again.
That's how...
we'll grow old together.

—Kyoko Honda
The Final Chapter

COMMENT

@mikanicecream: No matter how many years pass, this line has stayed in my mind. Whenever I remember *Furuba*, this is the line I always flash to first. I love these words, and I hope from the bottom of my heart the love of my life is like this. That's how emotionally attached I am to this scene. When I was a kid, I couldn't buy the collected volumes because I didn't have the money, but now I have the collector's editions, and rereading that scene still hits home. I can't even express how much I love that moment when Kyo and Tohru take their big step forward together.

Other Opinions

@kairi_12_: Just seeing the backs of the elderly Tohru-kun and Kyo-kun can make me happy. I truly love *Furuba*.

@oyster_lemon: There must be a lot of lines, but I suffer from memory loss, so I'll go with the one I can remember clearly and say the last line is the best.

This Line Too!

Please let her be loved
by many people.
Even if she gets lost...
Even if she makes mistakes...
let her live a life she can be proud of.
The kind of life that'll make people say
"You did your best" at the end...
Joyous times...sad times...
The cycle repeating itself, again and again.
That's how I want her to grow older.

—Kyoko Honda
Chapter 135

@iti_sousaku118: I cry every time I read this memorable scene. And then in the last scene, when Kyoko-san's wish comes true, I was overjoyed!!

@truth_bell06: Kyoko-san's words made me wail at the very end...

When snow melts, what does it become?

It becomes spring...!! No matter how cold it is now, spring will always come. It's magical, isn't it...?

—Hatori Sohma and Tohru Honda
Chapter 12

COMMENT

@rikka921: I can't count the number of times these words encouraged me.

Other Opinions
@miyu_k114: I read this scene when I was in elementary school, and it made me tear up.
@sA2RH4tTuXfki1d: I've loved this ever since I was little! Each character has their own personality, and the series is sensitive to that...I adore this manga! If I ever have a kid, I definitely want them to read this!

So choose me, Kyoko.

—Katsuya Honda
Chapter 91

COMMENT

@remamber5star: "So choose me, Kyoko." "It's your fault for being born late." Katsuya only appeared for a short while in a tale from the past, but this line made a huge impact. Unsurprising, since he's Tohru's dad!

Other Opinions
@sek146: I'm male, and I was a college student at the time—and reading this made my heart throb. I thought, "I wanna confess my love to someone like this!" (*´ω`*)
@ono_milk: I love too many lines to choose, but when Tohru's papa says to Tohru's mama, "So choose me, Kyoko," my heart beat so fast! I'm a Kyonkichi supporter.
@muginohosaki: Every time I read it, I wish, "Won't someone say that line to me?" and then I feel embarrassed. (//∇//)

Also from that Scene

...Choose me. If you still don't believe me, then I'll say it as many times as it takes to make you feel secure. But... I don't want my words to be wasted. So choose me, Kyoko.

@10karen01: That's a really straightforward proposal! I love his passionate feelings for Kyoko-san!

You shouldn't think... you can get away with anything just because you "love" someone. Because if that is what you think, I suggest you do some soul-searching. Directing an ever-increasing amount of one-sided love at someone becomes burdensome to that person, and at some point, you'll hurt them. Remember that.

—Megumi Hanajima
Chapter 29

COMMENT

@MukkunRou: Megumi-kun...is an adult.

Another Opinion
@sweetalice0214: Right now I really understand the meaning of these words......

She said people aren't born with a conscience. We're only born with "wants," she said, like appetite and material desires. In other words, survival instincts. The conscience is something that develops, like our bodies. It's our heart that grows inside of us. She said that's why there are different forms of kindness, depending on the person.

Everyone has desires from the moment they're born, so that's easy to understand. But kindness is something that each person has to craft for themselves. It's easily misinterpreted or taken for hypocrisy.

—Tohru Honda and Kyoko Honda
Chapter 4

COMMENT

@jiaotianl: Thanks to these words, my negative thinking turned into positive thinking. (*´ω`*)

Other Opinions
@_1kcn: I love Yuki-kun's kindness after this. Lines from the Hondas, mother and daughter, have saved me many times.
@416hw: Kyoko-san really is a wonderful person. These are especially memorable lines.

Also from that Scene

Tohru...
I want you to believe.
Anyone can doubt. That's easy.
Become the kind of girl who can believe in other people.
And I'm sure you will...
give someone strength.

@ryuka0118: Kyoko-san is cool and strong yet tenderhearted. She really is a wonderful person. I love her and Katsuya-san together.

Just as all good things... happy things, fun things... must come to an end, scary and sad things will also come to an end. Always.

—Tohru Honda
Chapter 122

COMMENT

@3737fun9: Even when I'm going through a rough time, if I recall Tohru-kun's words, I feel like I can hang in there.

Also from that Scene

Please live. Don't ever stop moving forward. Please...That's all I ask. Don't give up. Even if...I'm... no longer at your side...

@arashi006: Tohru-kun's kind feelings in that sad scene.
@chisatoka: As the final chapter approached, my tear glands gave way. I'll love *Furuba* my whole life!! Thank you, *Furuba*!!
@ichimaru41: I reread several volumes to find it, and now my tears won't stop. (´;ω;`)

The above comments were solicited on Twitter with the tweet: "Here's a 12-volume collector's edition completion memorial popularity contest!! Tell us your favorite line from *Furuba*!" Voting period: April 28–May 31, 2016, closing at midnight. The results are included here. We received many wonderful comments, a portion of them reprinted above. Also, some letters or symbols were left out due to printing difficulties. Thank you for understanding.

YES...

BUT...
...I FAILED PART OF THE MID-TERM.
IT'S JUST PATHETIC......

AH!
NOT AT ALL... UM...
I AM NOT...

MAYBE IT'LL FEEL DIFFERENT SEEING THEM HERE!

Tohru Honda

When first appeared: 1st year, Kaibara High School →
After graduation: Moved to a distant place with Kyo
Nicknames: Tohru-kun, Tohru
Family: Father (Katsuya Honda), mother (Kyoko Honda), both deceased; Living apart: Grandfather, uncle, aunt, male cousin, female cousin
Lives at Shigure Sohma's home

Clothing Concept

Natsuki Takaya Commentary

When choosing clothes, she goes for durability and how long they'll last over style, so her wardrobe is pretty plain. Simply put, she's unfashionable. (LOL) But recently she's had more money to spare, so she's been buying clothes that are a little cuter than before. Around Chapter 25, she wears a girlie-type (?) outfit, but that was a present from Shigure. He gives her a lot of presents. (I think we can all sympathize with Shigure's feelings there......) She did accept the maid outfit in Chapter 18, but in the end, Yuki and Kyo stopped her from ever wearing it. To this day, it lies dormant in Tohru's dresser.

—Excerpt from *Fan Book (Cat)*, 2005

Childhood

BAKI (CRACK)

Kyo Sohma

When first appeared: 1st year, Kaibara High School →
After graduation: Started working and training at the dojo of an acquaintance of Kazuma
Nicknames: Kyon-kyon, Kyonkichi
Family: Mother, deceased; Living apart: Father, foster father (Kazuma Sohma)
Lives at Shigure Sohma's home

Clothing Concept

In my humble opinion, out of all the male characters I've drawn, he looks the best in V-neck shirts...He likes rough clothes that are easy to move around in and don't require any maintenance, and he hates clothes that are tight around his neck. He doesn't wear any accessories except for the beads (and he only wears those because he has to). At the end of the day, he dislikes wearing anything that feels "annoying"—including socks. He liked the pants he was wearing during his first appearance, but they got torn up, so he had to throw them away......Sorry.

—Excerpt from *Fan Book (Cat)*, 2005

......

Childhood

...BEGIN TO SAY HOW MUCH...

CAT

...KINDA SICK MYSELF.

!

Yuki Sohma

When first appeared: 1st year, Kaibara High School →
After graduation: Went to a university far away
Nicknames: Yun-yun, the Prince
Origin of name: "Yuki" just popped into my head
Family: Living apart: Father, mother, older brother (Ayame Sohma)
Lives at Shigure Sohma's home

Clothing Concept

He doesn't wear Chinese-style clothes because he likes them; it's more that *I* like Chinese clothes. But I think they suit the androgynous Yuki well...Do you agree? He especially likes sleek, light shirts, and he doesn't like accessories at all. Also, for Yuki's and Kyo's clothes, I wanted them to be at odds with each other on that too, along the lines of, "I wouldn't be caught dead in the clothes you wear! Sooo not my style." You get the idea.

—Excerpt from *Fan Book (Cat)*, 2005

RAT

...I'LL KIDNAP YOU...
...SO BE PREPARED.

Childhood

YOU HAVE ANY IDEA HOW WORRIED EVERYONE IS?

IF YOU'RE A REAL MAN, YOU'LL ANSWER THE CALL OF ANY CHALLENGE...
...KITTY CAT...

...RIN.

Hatsuharu Sohma

When first appeared: 3rd year, middle school →
Currently: 2nd-year student at Kaibara High School
Nicknames: Haru, Haa-kun, Haru-nii
Origin of name: The first month of the lunar calendar (the beginning of spring), *Hatsuharu*
Family: Father, mother
Lives on the "inside" of the Sohma compound

Clothing Concept

He used to dress similar to Kyo, but Isuzu's influence made him adopt a flashier style, which he's grown to like......Like Momiji, Haru has a lot of clothes and spends a considerable amount of money on them. He especially likes leather goods (and thus likes winter).

—Excerpt from *Fan Book (Cat)*, 2005

Childhood

OX

I CAN TRY HARD...
...BECAUSE MY MOM...
...AND ALL OF YOU...

Kisa Sohma

When first appeared: 1st year, private middle school →
Currently: 3rd-year student at private middle school
Nickname: Sacchan
Origin of name: The second month of the lunar calendar, *Kisaragi*
Family: Father, mother
Lives on the "inside" of the Sohma compound

TIGER

Clothing Concept

She likes to wear dresses. I'd like to have her wear more feminine dresses with lots of frills, but it seems Kisa isn't interested in that kind of thing yet. (LOL) (Although I do put her in dresses like that when I've got color pages and such.) She doesn't like gaudy colors.

—Excerpted from *Fan Book (Cat)*, 2005

Momiji Sohma

When first appeared: 3rd year, private middle school →
Currently: 2nd-year student at Kaibara High School
Nickname: Momicchi
Origin of name: The ninth month of the lunar calendar, *Momijizuki*
Family: Living apart: Papa, mama (memories of him buried), little sister (Momo)
Lives on the "inside" of the Sohma compound

Clothing Concept

He likes to wear Lolita clothes, so I just let him do his thing. You do you, Momiji! He has a ton of clothes, so storing them all has to be a nightmare. (In fact, I wonder if he even remembers them all…) He has outfits made for him at Ayame's shop once in a while too. He has a particular fondness for poofy bloomers. But I also think he looks good (as the artist, am I allowed to say that?) in the male school uniform.

—Excerpt from *Fan Book (Cat)*, 2005

Sieh do!!
Welch ein Glück!!

WHAT SHOULD I DO?
I'M SO HAPPY...

RABBIT

CON-
GRATULA-
TIONS...

Hatori Sohma

The Sohma family doctor
Nicknames: Haa-san, Harii, Tori-san
Origin of name: The fourth month of the lunar calendar, *Konohatorizuki*
Family: Father (deceased), mother (deceased)
Lives on the "inside" of the Sohma compound

Clothing Concept

It's not that he has any great love for suits, he just likes that they don't require much thought to decide on. In fact, he has his housekeeper pick out his daily suit (something Kana did for him when they were still together). Eventually, someone is bound to give him an earful about that attitude.

—Excerpt from *Fan Book (Cat)*, 2005

...
THANK YOU.

High School Days

STOP ACTING LIKE AN IDIOT. LET'S GO.

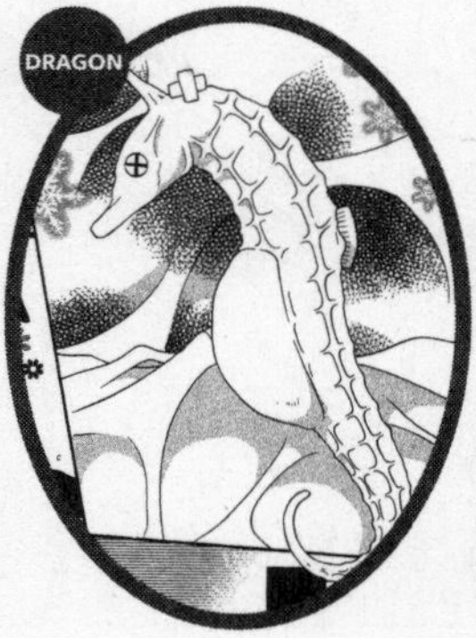
DRAGON

Ayame Sohma

Clothing designer and owner of "Ayame," a custom clothing and handicrafts shop
Nicknames: Aaya, Bossman, Aya-kun, Aya-nii
Origin of name: The fifth month of the lunar calendar, *Ayamezuki*
Family: Father, mother, younger brother (Yuki Sohma)
Lives outside the Sohma family compound in a home attached to his shop

Clothing Concept

Since his younger brother wears Chinese-style clothing, I decided that meant Ayame was the same way. Not really a decision I gave much thought...so recently, I've been questioning that choice. (LOL) When Ayame wants to wear a certain type of outfit, he sketches it on paper, and then Mine makes it for him. As a matter of fact, he won't let anyone else make his clothes! He loves outrageous and magnificent clothing, especially in red and gold.

—Excerpt from *Fan Book (Cat)*, 2005

EVERY-ONE...
NO NEED TO FRET, GURE-SAN...
EVEN IF THE WHOLE WORLD TURNED AGAINST YOU, I WOULD REMAIN YOUR STEADFAST ALLY......

WELL HELLO, EVERYONE...
FORGIVE ME FOR BEING LATE......!

SNAKE

High School Days

...I'M "BOTTOM" ALL THE WAYYY!!

CHARACTER CONTESTS

Hana to Yume Issue 4, 2000

2nd Place
Tohru Honda
11,922 votes

1st Place
Kyo Sohma
17,218 votes

3rd Place
Yuki Sohma
11,187 votes

Ranking	Character	Votes
4	Hatori Sohma	6,885
5	Shigure Sohma	5,614
6	Hatsuharu Sohma	5,589
7	Ayame Sohma	3,684
8	Momiji Sohma	1,654
9	Saki Hanajima	1,581
10	Kagura Sohma	1,184
11	Kisa Sohma	975
12	Kazuma Sohma	613

Ranking	Character	Votes
13	Akito Sohma	525
14	Megumi Hanajima	301
15	Kyoko Honda	267
16	Arisa Uotani	182
17	Mogeta	123
18	Hot-Spring Mistress	89
19	Tohru's Grandfather	67
20	Mayuko Shiraki	42

Hana to Yume Issue 17, 2004

2nd Place
Tohru Honda
4,680 votes

1st Place
Kyo Sohma
7,725 votes

3rd Place
Yuki Sohma
3,134 votes

Ranking	Character	Votes
4	Hatori Sohma	1,498
5	Hatsuharu Sohma	1,224
6	Momiji Sohma	1,193
7	Kakeru Manabe	1,025
8	Ayame Sohma	928
9	Kureno Sohma	798
10	Shigure Sohma	741
11	Isuzu Sohma	715
12	Saki Hanajima	534

Ranking	Character	Votes
13	Ritsu Sohma	527
14	Kisa Sohma	495
15	Machi Kuragi	358
16	Hiro Sohma	331
17	Kazuma Sohma	254
18	Akito Sohma	252
19	Arisa Uotani	223
20	Kagura Sohma	211

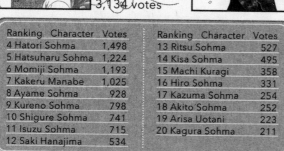

About the Character Contests:
First contest announced and votes solicited in *Hana to Yume* Issue 4, 2000, with results posted in *Hana to Yume* Issue 8, 2000.
Second contest announced and votes solicited in *Hana to Yume* Issue 17, 2004, with results posted in *Hana to Yume* Issue 22, 2004.

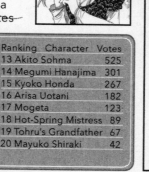

Hana to Yume Issue 24, 2006

4th Place
Kisa Sohma
1,288 votes

1st Place
Kyo Sohma
5,313 votes

5th Place
Hatsuharu Sohma
1,216 votes

6th Place
Hatori Sohma
1,214 votes

7th Place
Momiji Sohma
1,080 votes

8th Place
Shigure Sohma
773 votes

2nd Place
Tohru Honda
3,322 votes

9th Place
Ayame Sohma
730 votes

Ranking	Character	Votes
10	Kakeru Manabe	725
11	Akito Sohma	713
12	Saki Hanajima	683
13	Hiro Sohma	559
14	Isuzu Sohma	467
15	Machi Kuragi	458
16	Kureno Sohma	299
17	Kyoko Honda	272
18	Katsuya Honda	250
18	Kagura Sohma	250
20	Arisa Uotani	214
21	Ritsu Sohma	126
22	Kazuma Sohma	104
23	Mogeta	59
24	Megumi Hanajima	41
25	Mayuko Shiraki	39
26	Tohru's Grandpa	35
27	Naoto Sakuragi	29
28	Motoko Minagawa	26
29	Kimi Toudou	24
29	Friends	24
31	Ren Sohma	15

3rd Place
Yuki Sohma
2,497 votes

Third contest announced in *Hana to Yume* Issue 24, 2006, with votes solicited in the magazine as well as on the *Hana to Yume* homepage, and results were published in *Fan Book (Banquet)*.
All three popularity contests had different forms of solicitations and tabulating methods.

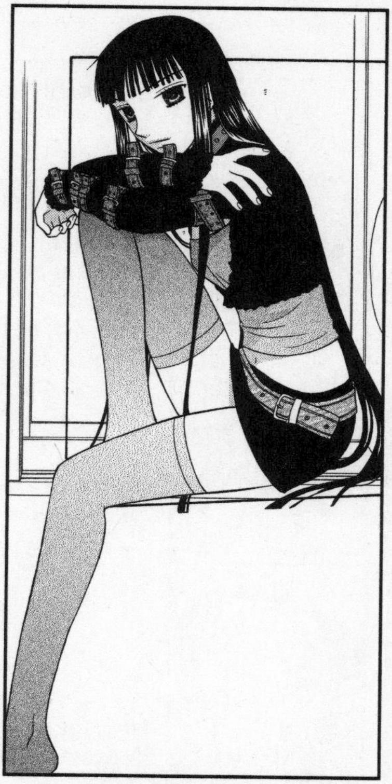

Isuzu Sohma

When first appeared: 1st year, private girls' school →
Currently: Graduated
Nickname: Rin
Origin of name: The sixth month of the lunar calendar, *Isuzukuretsuki*
Family: Living apart: Father, mother
Lives at Kagura Sohma's house but also often stays with Kazuma Sohma

Clothing Concept

As a child, she always wore cute outfits, so her flashy style is partially a rebellion against that. It's a combination of rejection and stubbornness. But now that her long hair has been lopped off and she's cleared one big emotional hurdle, I have the feeling her interests will change a bit.

—Excerpt from *Fan Book (Cat)*, 2005

Childhood

YOU'VE GOT A FUNNY SENSE OF LOGIC, HARU.

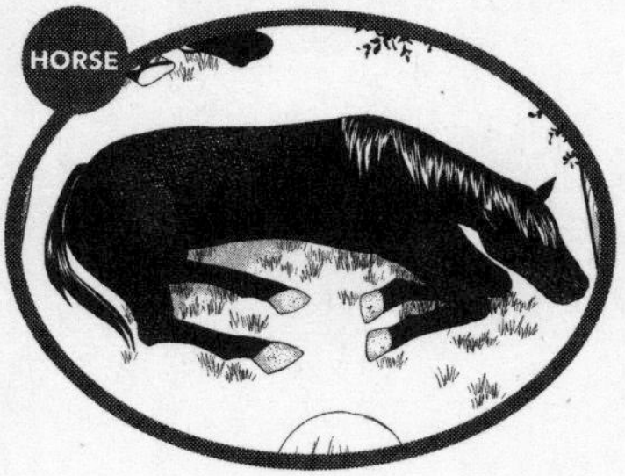
HORSE

HMM...

Hiro Sohma

When first appeared: 6th grade, elementary school →
Currently: 2nd-year middle school student
Nicknames: Hiro, Hii-kun
Origin of name: The seventh month of the lunar calendar, *Fumihirogezuki*
Family: Father, mother (Satsuki Sohma), younger sister (Hinata Sohma)
Lives on the "inside" of the Sohma compound

Clothing Concept

He hates sloppiness, so he always takes good care of his clothes. It's like he wears well-tailored clothing. He doesn't care for accessories, except for small items (?) that accent his clothes. Therefore, as with Haru, I think Hiro likes winter clothes.

—Excerpt from *Fan Book (Cat)*, 2005

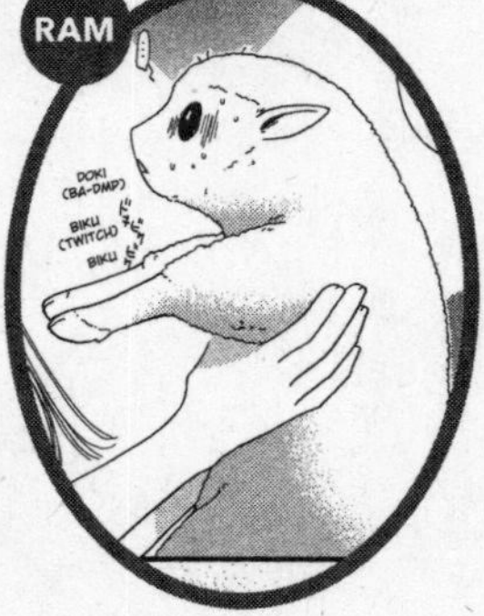
RAM
DOKI (BA-DMP)
BIKU (TWITCH)
BIKU

I WOULD BE SO HAPPY...

THANK YOU SO MUCH...

AHHH...
GOD... BUDDHA...

Ritsu Sohma

When first appeared: 3rd-year university student
Nickname: Ricchan-san
Origin of name: The ninth month of the lunar calendar, *Odakaritsuzuki*
Family: Father, mother (the hostess of the Sohma-owned hot-spring inn)
Lives on the "outside" of the Sohma compound

Clothing Concept

He wears chic skirts, but it seems kimonos (of course with long sleeves) are his favorite thing to wear. He's known at his college for dressing in women's clothes. When he does wear men's clothing, it's often a suit. Those suits may be more aesthetically pleasing than the suits Hatori wears... Just a little bit...

—Excerpt from *Fan Book (Cat)*, 2005

Childhood

MY HEART ACHES.

MONKEY

NOOOOOOOOO!

Kureno Sohma

Attendant to the head of the Sohma family →
Later: Left the Sohma compound and moved to a rural town far away
Nickname: Kureno
Origin of name: The third month of the lunar calendar, *Kurenoharu*
Family: Father, mother
Lives in the Sohma mansion

Clothing Concept

He avoids wearing white shirts (except when he has to, like his high school uniform). I have the feeling he avoids the color white altogether. He wants to blend in as much as possible, so this aversion could be an expression of his desire to go unnoticed. Also, he doesn't often wear suits—that would make him and Hatori-san a bit too similar, don't you think...? (LOL)

—Excerpt from *Fan Book (Cat)*, 2005

Teenage Years

ROOSTER

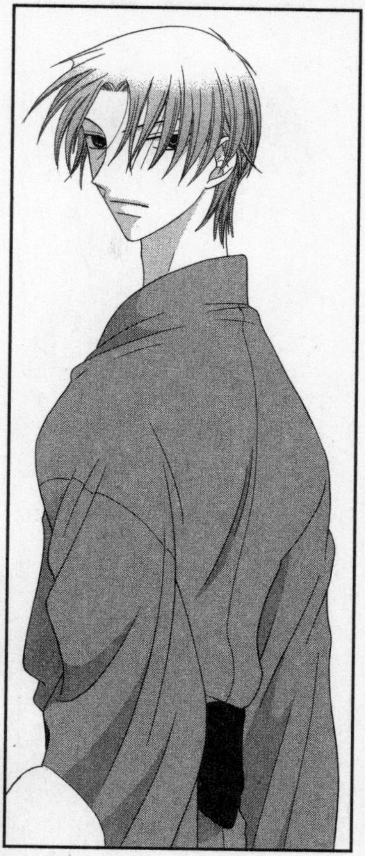

Shigure Sohma

Stay-at-home author →
Later: Attendant to the head of the Sohma family
Nicknames: Gure-san, Shii-chan, Gure-nii
Origin of name: The tenth month of the lunar calendar, *Shigurezuki*
Family: Father, mother
Lives in a house outside the Sohma compound

Clothing Concept

He got this idea in his head that novelists are supposed to wear kimonos—so he did, without putting any more thought into it or effort to make it look elegant. Before becoming a novelist (in other words, when he was still living in the Sohma compound), he wore casual shirts and jeans, but even that careless, casual look was an act, as if he wanted to show people that he didn't care what he wore.

—Excerpt from *Fan Book (Cat)*, 2005

DOG

ARE YOU...
...STUPID?

High School Days

YOU WOULD CRY IF I TOLD YOU, KYO-KUN ......
...so it stays my secret. ♡

BOAR

Childhood

KYO-CHAN ...

WHO'S SHOWIN' WHO NO MERCY!?

Kagura Sohma

When first appeared: 1st-year, private women's junior college →
Currently: Has found a job after graduating
Nickname: Kagura
Origin of name: The eleventh month of the lunar calendar, *Kagurazuki*
Family: Father, mother
Lives on the "inside" of the Sohma compound

Clothing Concept

She wears awfully childish, cute clothes for a young woman who's almost twenty. Her reasoning is that she has a baby face that matches the clothes, but she also secretly worries she won't seem like a good match for Kyo if she wears more mature clothing. Kagura made her cat backpack by hand and has several spares (?). Her bedroom is crammed full of cat stuffed animals, all of them orange. Her room is orange too...which sounds like it would be hard on the eyes...

—Excerpt from *Fan Book (Cat)*, 2005

Akito Sohma

Head of the Sohma family
Nicknames: Akito, Aa-chan
Family: Father (Akira Sohma), deceased; mother (Ren Sohma)
Lives in the Sohma mansion

Clothing Concept

She wears kimonos almost exclusively, which is kind of odd...When it comes to Western-style clothes, she likes plain outfits. Or—I guess it's more that she hates gaudily decorated clothes, not to mention that she dislikes having her skin show. Even though she doesn't seem to mind if parts of her bare skin show when she's wearing a kimono... (LOL)

—Excerpt from *Fan Book (Cat)*, 2005

...ALL OF YOU.

WAS THAT SO WRONG?

Childhood

BEST COUPLE & COMBINATION CONTEST

Hana to Yume Issue 24, 2006

1st Place
Tohru Honda & Kyo Sohma
1,545 votes

...YEAH.
I'M BACK.
I DON'T WANT TO JUST TAKE ANYMORE.
I LOVE YOU.
I DON'T WANT TO TRAMPLE ON ANYTHING...
...EVER AGAIN.
...I WAS HOPING...
...THAT WE COULD BE TOGETHER FOREVER SOMEHOW. SOMEWHERE. BUT...

2nd Place
Yuki Sohma & Machi Kuragi
296 votes

SO THIS IS...
...WHERE YOU'VE BEEN.

3rd Place
Kisa Sohma & Hiro Sohma
184 votes

...
...ME TOO.
IT'S MY FAULT.
...I'M SORRY...
I'M REALLY SORRY...
I'M SORRY.
I HAVE TO...
...BECOME...

4th Place
Hatsuharu Sohma
& Isuzu Sohma
166 votes

...DO YOU THINK I JUST FEEL SORRY FOR YOU?
THAT'S —
I LOVE YOU.
THAT'S NOT IT!
AND I...
...WANT YOU.
RIN, DO YOU...
...NOT WANT ME?
YOU DON'T WANNA BE TOGETHER?
......
...

5th Place
Shigure Sohma
& Akito Sohma
161 votes

...HERE.
...FOR ETERNITY.
I MISSED YOU.

Ranking	Character	Votes
6	Tohru Honda & Yuki Sohma	134
7	Katsuya Honda & Kyoko Honda	101
8	Shigure Sohma & Hatori Sohma & Ayame Sohma	80
9	Kureno Sohma & Arisa Uotani	75
10	Yuki Sohma & Kakeru Manabe	60
11	Tohru Honda & Saki Hanajima & Arisa Uotani	49
12	Tohru Honda & Kisa Sohma	46
13	Tohru Honda & Yuki Sohma & Kyo Sohma	43
14	Hatori Sohma & Mayuko Shiraki	39
15	Yuki Sohma & Kyo Sohma	32
16	Tohru Honda & Momiji Sohma	31
17	Yuki Sohma & Hatsuharu Sohma	27
18	Yuki Sohma & Ayame Sohma	24
19	Saki Hanajima & Kazuma Sohma	20
19	Kyo Sohma & Arisa Uotani	20
21	Kyo Sohma & Kagura Sohma	15
21	Tohru Honda & Isuzu Sohma	15
23	Kyo Sohma & Kazuma Sohma	14
23	Hatsuharu Sohma & Kisa Sohma	14
25	Arisa Uotani & Saki Hanajima	13
26	Shigure Sohma & Ayame Sohma	12
27	Kyo Sohma & Saki Hanajima	11
28	Akito Sohma & Kureno Sohma	10
28	Tohru Honda & Hatori Sohma	10
30	Ayame Sohma & Mine Kuramae	9

About the Best Couple & Combination Contest: Votes were solicited in *Hana to Yume* Issue 24, 2006, as well as on the *Hana to Yume* homepage. The results were first published in *Fan Book (Banquet)*.

...I CAN FEEL AT EASE IN THIS "RESPECTABLE WORLD"...
...BECAUSE I'VE GOT TOHRU.

IF IT'S JUST A SCOLDING THAT YOU NEED...

Arisa Uotani

When first appeared: 1st year, Kaibara High School →
After graduation: Followed Kureno, got a job in a rural town far away
Nicknames: Uo-chan, Delinquent
Family: Father, mother (missing)
Lives with her father in an apartment

Clothing Concept

She likes form-fitting outfits. When she was in a gang, she always wore clothes that covered up her skin, but since reforming (?), it seems she's been choosing outfits that are on the risqué side. Kyoko-san was a major influence on Uo-chan's taste in clothes, but she still prefers long skirts (a shame because she has nice legs).

—Excerpt from *Fan Book (Cat)*, 2005

Middle School Days

GO (RUMBLE)
GO
GO
GO
PINK...
...IS TOHRU-KUN'S...
GO
GO
GO
GO
GO

Saki Hanajima

When first appeared: 1st year, Kaibara High School →
After graduation: Became the cook at Kazuma's dojo
Nicknames: Hana-chan, Demon Queen
Family: Father, mother, grandmother, younger brother (Megumi Hanajima)
Lives with her family in a house

Clothing Concept

Outside school, she only wears black. If you open her closet, the blackness inside is like an artistic masterpiece. She's also been painting her nails black too since middle school. Her favorite ensemble is a chic, elegant black dress with a black cape that matches her brother's (her grandmother made the capes).

—Excerpt from *Fan Book (Cat)*, 2005

...LET ME SEE...
FOR THE TIME BEING...

Childhood

...SO I'D LIKE TO PUT OFF TELLING YOU...
...FOR JUST A LITTLE LONGER.
THAT OKAY?

......SO?

KUWA (GLARE)
...DON'T YOU THINK HAVING A DISCUSSION ABOUT COLORS...

Kakeru Manabe

Nicknames: Nabe, Vice President, Flying Pot-kun, Shou
Family: Mother, half sister (Machi Kuragi)
Lives in an apartment with his mother—who's usually out, so he actually stays with Komaki half the time.

......

Machi Kuragi

Nickname: Machi
Family: Lives apart: Father, mother, younger brother, half brother (Kakeru Manabe)
Lives alone in a condo. She was kicked out of her house after her parents mistakenly suspected her of trying to murder her baby brother.

...HERE IS SOMEONE WHO'S PRAISING ME.

Katsuya Honda

Died from an illness when Tohru was just a toddler
Family: Father, mother (deceased), younger sister

Kyoko Honda

Maiden name: Kyoko Katsunuma
Nicknames: Red Butterfly, Ms. No Eyebrows
Died in a traffic accident when Tohru was a 1st-year high school student
Family: (Estranged) Father, mother
Married Katsuya Honda after graduating from middle school

Middle School Days

THERE'S STUFF EVERYWHERE, HA!

BEST-STORY CONTEST

Hana to Yume Issue 24, 2006. Comments originally published in *Fan Book (Banquet)*.

1st Place Chapter 136

YOU...
MORE THAN YOU KNOW...
SO...
...IT'S GONNA BE OKAY. IT'S NOT LIKE WE'RE LEAVING FOREVER.
...EVERY-ONE...
...LOVES YOU TOO.
...THIS IS JUST THE BEGINNING...
...OF A NEW BANQUET.
...RIGHT?

I'm glad the final chapter came in first place... (LOL) Thank you very much. Again, as I keep saying, I had the final chapter in mind while writing and drawing the first chapter, so *Furuba* has always been moving toward this finale. I don't know what I would've done if it hadn't ranked first! (LOL) When Yuki calls her just "Tohru" at the end, without the need for an honorific, you should feel a flood of emotions... Well, maybe I'm overdoing it, but I hope you felt something in your heart. Of course, even aside from that, if something in this series touched your heart, I'm overjoyed.

2nd Place Chapter 33

......TOHRU...
TOHRU...
...BUT JUST LIKE THAT...

I think Kyo's popularity might have become unshakeable after this chapter. This is also when the relationship between Tohru and Kyo starts getting serious (I'm moved when I think of how lovey-dovey they are now). Maybe that's why this chapter had so much reader support to the very end. Actually, there's another personal reason this chapter was significant for me. While working on the manuscript, I had a fever of nearly 104°F! I was burning up so much that I don't even remember how I put the finishing touches on. Good job, me! (LOL)

3rd Place Chapter 123

DO YOU SERIOUSLY THINK...
...SHE'D BE JUST AS HAPPY IF IT WERE ME!?
YOU NEED TO REALIZE THERE ARE SOME THINGS...
...ONLY YOU CAN DO!
SO QUIT MAKING HER CRY!
GET YOUR HEAD OUT OF YOUR ASS!
AND GET YOUR ACT TOGETHER!!!

This is another chapter I planned out well in advance, so I'm happy it ranked third. I wanted these two to have their last fight like this. Yuki-kun really lets Kyo-kun have it, but by this point Yuki is even more aware of his admiration for Kyo than he's ever been——so when Kyo beats him to the punch with his own confession, it doubles Yuki's frustration. (LOL) It makes Yuki snap! (LOL) After this, it's not like they're going to become best buds, but I hope you'll agree that the kind of relationship they will have is a good one. I have a feeling their kids will become good friends.

 About the Best-Story Contest: Votes were solicited in *Hana to Yume* Issue 24, 2006, as well as on the *Hana to Yume* homepage. The results were first published in *Fan Book (Banquet)*.

BEST-STORY CONTEST

Hana to Yume Issue 24, 2006

4th Place Chapter 88

WHAT ARE YOU SITTIN' HERE BROODING FOR, GRUMPYPANTS? THIS SHINDIG IS FOR YOU.
GO FIND YOURSELF A MAIDEN FAIR.
STUFF IT. I AIN'T INTERESTED. GO FIND YOUR OWN MAIDEN FAIR.
SEE, THIS IS WHY YOU'RE GONNA DIE A VIRGIN.
HEY!
YOU OUGHTA RUN OUT TO THE STORE RIGHT NOW AND BUY YOURSELF SOME "DIGNITY"!!
EXCUSE ME!?
I SAID IT BECAUSE I WAS WORRIED ABOUT YOU! WITH THAT ATTITUDE, YOU'RE THE ONE WHO SHOULD GO OUT—TO BUY SOME "COURTESY"!!
HOW CAN YOU SAY A LINE LIKE THAT AND NOT BLUSH!!?
The prince's friend, a fellow prince, tried cordial persuasion, but alas, it was not enough to spur the prince to dance.

The only reason I had Hana-chan play Cinderella instead of Tohru was I thought it'd be funnier with Hana-chan. (LOL) Even more so if Kyo-kun played her romantic partner. Those two don't get along at all, and yet, on some level, they do. I secretly loved Uo-chan's princely style. Afterward, this chapter became a drama CD, and I rewrote the script for that. It was pretty difficult, especially when the characters have to explain what I could just show with art in the manga. If you're interested, please listen to the CD.

5th Place Chapter 122

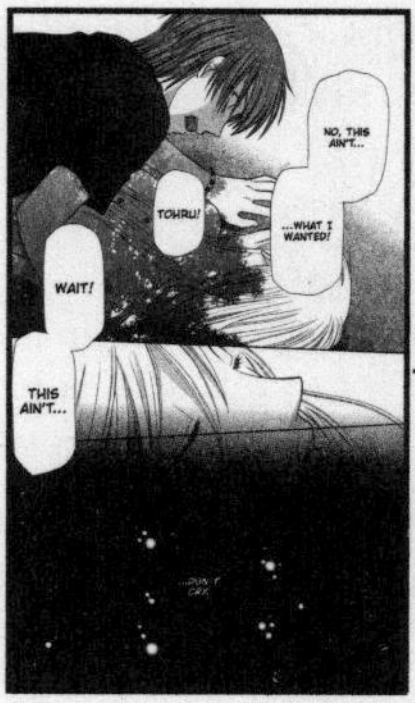
NO, THIS AIN'T...
...WHAT I WANTED!
TOHRU!
WAIT!
THIS AIN'T...

I was worried when I realized how shocked Kyo is at seeing Tohru after she falls the cliff. He was a lot more distressed than I'd thought he'd be, back when I dreamed up this scene. I was in trouble—even more so than with Chapter 33! I thought, "Will he really disappear this time?!" (LOL) In desperation, I had Tohru wake up a bit to set him straight. And actually, the kissing scene at the end wasn't part of the original plan either. It was almost like Kyo does it all on his own. What am I talking about, since I'm the one who wrote it? You may be asking me that right now, but sometimes that kind of weird experience just happens.

6th Place Chapter 129

WE'RE ALREADY HOLDIN' HANDS.
I COULD HEAR THOSE WORDS...

This is the culmination of their story. That's right—they finally got together! (LOL) I bet a lot of readers were waiting for this moment, so I endeavored to bring them together in a way I wouldn't regret. After all, it would've been kind of boring if they'd just said "I love you" and then kissed, right...? As I was working on this chapter, I realized once again that while Kyo-kun has a bashful side, he can also be serious when the time comes. Once he decides on something, I think he stops being embarrassed about it. He becomes very straightforward.

7th Place Chapter 23

This is another chapter that the fans have supported for a looong time. Getting to see a flashback to little Momiji makes me nostalgic. To be honest, so much time has passed since I worked on this chapter that my memories are fuzzy, so my apologies... The series ends after Momiji gets tall and masculine, but I kind of wanted to keep it going 'til he gets a girlfriend...Nah, that wouldn't have worked. All I can do is imagine what could have been... (LOL)

8th Place Chapter 76

These days, people don't remember historic sayings like "Let's create a wonderful country, Kamakura Shogunate," do they? Times change so quickly...I remember this chapter being really difficult to do. It was tough getting everybody on the same page! But maybe my suffering was worth it for Kyo and Tohru's scene. (LOL) And I also like the bit at the end with Mayu-chan-sensei. Maybe that's out of character for me, and it should be embarrassing—but I already said it, so... (LOL)

9th Place Chapter 1

The nostalgic first chapter. The beginning of the journey for Tohru and the others. Yeah. This is the all-important "Chapter 1." It's a memorable chapter also because my storyboards got the editorial okay the first time around (without any changes). When the anime version came out, I watched the first episode many times. Both the manga and anime make me feel nostalgic, like they're both my treasures. But if I dare say now—it blew me away that they slapped on a "To Be Continued" right when Tohru's future romantic partner, Kyo, makes his entrance. (LOL) It's great how he comes crashing in through the ceiling too. (LOL) You're hogging the spotlight, Kyo-kun.

10th Place Chapter 120

I don't want to interfere with readers' enjoyment of this chapter, so I'll refrain from picking at it, but while working on it, I was stumped over how to do a good job expressing Tohru-kun's once-in-a-lifetime display of guts. And Akito-san acted very differently than I'd first planned, so that was a major upset. All in my head, of course. (LOL) I was really busy back then. Also, I was a little worried that Kyo-kun's behavior in this chapter would make readers hate him, but instead you all watched over him kindly. I appreciate that.

Rank	Chapter	Rank	Chapter	Rank	Chapter	Rank	Chapter	Rank	Chapter
11	Chapter 101	17	Chapter 135	23	Chapter 17	29	Chapter 4	29	Chapter 106
12	Chapter 12	18	Chapter 51	23	Chapter 131	29	Chapter 41	29	Chapter 111
13	Chapter 121	19	Chapter 125	23	Chapter 132	29	Chapter 46		
14	Chapter 130	20	Chapter 74	26	Chapter 28	29	Chapter 62		
15	Chapter 124	21	Chapter 6	26	Chapter 100	29	Chapter 98		
16	Chapter 109	21	Chapter 92	26	Chapter 102	29	Chapter 103		

FRUITS BASKET'S HISTORY OF HAPPENINGS

REVIEW

A visual of the events that occurred in *Fruits Basket*, in chronological order!

Legend: (onigiri mark) → This mark indicates the general year of the event is unknown.

(1) → The circled number is the number of the chapter in which the event occurred.

Around the Honda Family	Time	Around the Sohma Family
	Long, long ago	
	(onigiri mark) (131)	Thirteen animals accept invitations from a god to attend banquets. The god proposes that they become connected through an "eternal bond" that shall survive even death. Only the Cat rejects that bond.
	Before Tohru was born	
	(onigiri mark) (115)	Akira, the head of the Sohma family, chooses his attendant, Ren, to be his bride.

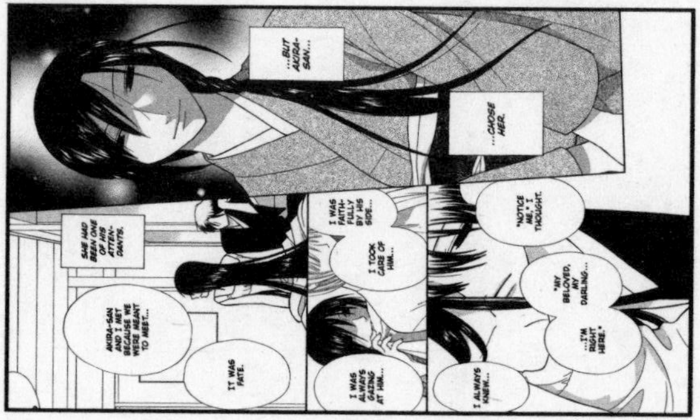

...BUT AKIRA-SAN...
...CHOSE HER.
SHE HAD BEEN ONE OF HIS ATTENDANTS.
AKIRA-SAN AND I MET BECAUSE WE WERE MEANT TO MEET...
IT WAS FATE.
I WAS FAITHFULLY BY HIS SIDE...
I TOOK CARE OF HIM...
I WAS ALWAYS GAZING AT HIM...
"NOTICE ME," I THOUGHT.
"MY BELOVED, MY DARLING...
...I'M RIGHT HERE."
I ALWAYS KNEW...

90 91 92 Middle school student Kyoko Katsunuma meets Katsuya Honda. After she graduates middle school, they get married.

SO CHOOSE ME...
...KYOKO.
KATSUYA...
DO YOU HAVE A LOLITA COMPLEX...?
...WHERE'D YOU PICK UP THAT PHRASE?
IT'S YOUR FAULT...
...FOR BEING BORN LATE.

98 115 Ren becomes pregnant with Akito. Shigure, Hatori, Ayame, and Kureno realize the god of the zodiac is going to be born again and pay Ren a visit.

16 Shigure realizes Ren is pregnant and that he already has feelings for Akito. He begins thinking that he wants a monopoly on Akito.

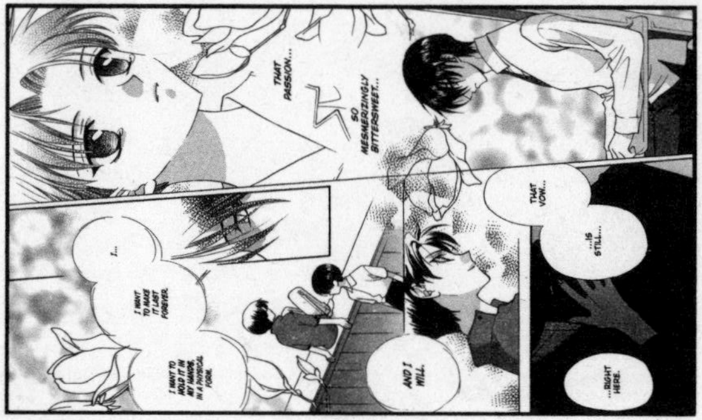
I...
I WANT TO MAKE IT LAST FOREVER.
I WANT TO HOLD IT IN MY HANDS, IN A PHYSICAL FORM.
THAT PASSION...
SO MESMERIZINGLY BITTERSWEET...
AND I WILL.
THAT VOW...
...IS STILL...
...RIGHT HERE.

Before Tohru goes to elementary school

117 Akira, the head of the Sohma family, dies. As the next head of the family, Akito inherits full authority. Akira's dying words are "And our child was even a 'special being'...That's proof that the two of us were 'special' too, isn't it...?"

92 Tohru is born.

TOHRU!

Around the Honda Family	Time	Around the Sohma Family
		(117) The head Sohma maid gives Akito a small box that she claims contains "Akira's soul."
Katsuya Honda dies. (1) (92) (93)	Tohru is 3 years old	
Kyoko leaves Tohru at home alone, intending to "follow" Katsuya. (70) (92) (93) (109)	Sometime after the funeral	

Your husband has been worried about you all this time.
He says you can't keep crying like this.
He's watching over you and wants the best for you, so you need to pull yourself together...
I WANT TO SEE HIM TOO...
I WANT TO GO SEE HIM...
WHERE ARE YOU?
WHERE DO I NEED TO GO TO FIND YOU AGAIN?

YOU REMEMBER WHAT HE SAID?
...?
"I'LL BE WITH YOU."
WHAT'S INSIDE?
THAT IS THE DUTY AKIRA-SAN GAVE TO YOU, THE ONE HE LOVED MOST OF ALL.
...AND, HERE...
YOU MUST TEACH HER THAT IN THE SOHMA FAMILY...
...YOUR ROLE AS THE ONE WHO RULES OVER THE SPIRITS IS SACRED.
AS LONG AS YOU HAVE THIS...
...AKIRA-SAN BELONGS TO YOU ALONE!

Yuki begins living with Akito at the main house. To his parents, it's like giving the head of the family a human sacrifice. (20) (47) (54) (58) (72) (84)

(109) After Kyoko disappears

Trying to imitate her father, Tohru learns to speak politely.

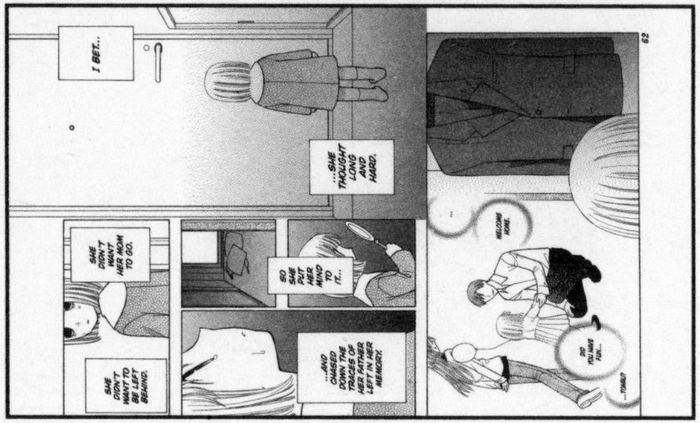
I BET...
...SHE THOUGHT LONG AND HARD.
SHE DIDN'T WANT HER MOM TO GO.
SHE DIDN'T WANT TO BE LEFT BEHIND.
SO SHE PUT HER MIND TO IT...
...AND CHASED DOWN THE TRACES OF HER FATHER LEFT IN HER MEMORY.
...
WELCOME HOME.
DID YOU HAVE FUN...
...TOHRU?
62

(68)(31) Kagura and Kyo become friends. After that, one day while playing together, Kagura sees Kyo's "true form."

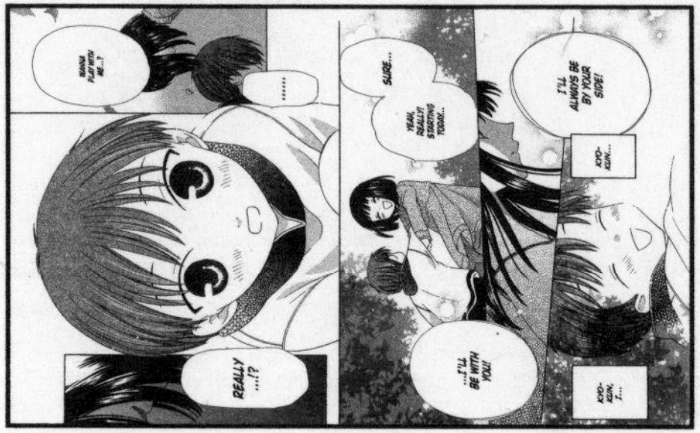
WANNA PLAY WITH ME...?
......
REALLY ...!?
SURE...
YEAH, REALLY! STARTING TODAY...
...I'LL BE WITH YOU!
I'LL ALWAYS BE BY YOUR SIDE!
KYO-KUN...
KYO-KUN, I...

Kyo is 4-5 years old

(126)(119)(109)(93)(63)(62)(58)(34)(33)(32) Kyo's mother commits suicide. People believe it's because she gave birth to the Cat, but the true cause was her husband abusing her for giving birth to the Cat. Kazuma takes Kyo in and raises him as his own.

SHUT UP...
THE BOY DOESN'T CRY.
EVEN THOUGH HIS OWN MOTHER DIED...
HE'S THE ONE WHO DROVE HER TO SUICIDE!
SHUT YOUR MOUTHS...
I DIDN'T DO IT!!
IT AIN'T MY FAULT!!
YES.

Kureno's curse is broken. (97)(96)(95)

Akito's world begins to crumble. (117)(84)

Around the Honda Family	Time	Around the Sohma Family

Tohru enters elementary school

(63)(90)(93)(119)(120) — Kyo meets Kyoko Honda.

...I WONDER...
...HOW LOST YOU'LL GET.
HOW MUCH TIME IT'LL TAKE...
...BEFORE YOU FIND YOUR ANSWER...

Yuki is in 2nd grade

(2)(84)(95) — Yuki makes his first friends, but when they see him transform into a rat, Hatori erases their memories.

(84)(85)(86)(87)(119) — Yuki finds Kyo's baseball cap.

AH...
H-HERE...

Tohru is 6-7 years old

(1) (7) (24) (53) (85) — Tohru gets lost because boys from her elementary school were bullying her. Early the next morning, a boy wearing a cap (Yuki) helps her.

...BUT EACH TIME...
...THE MYSTERIOUS BOY...
...WOULD WAIT FOR ME.
....
THE NEXT THING I KNEW...
...I WAS IN FRONT OF MY HOUSE.
THE BOY WAS NOWHERE TO BE SEEN.
THE ONLY TRACE OF HIM WAS THIS HAT.

(24) (53) (59) (85) — Yuki slips out of the main house early in the morning and helps the lost Tohru find her way home.

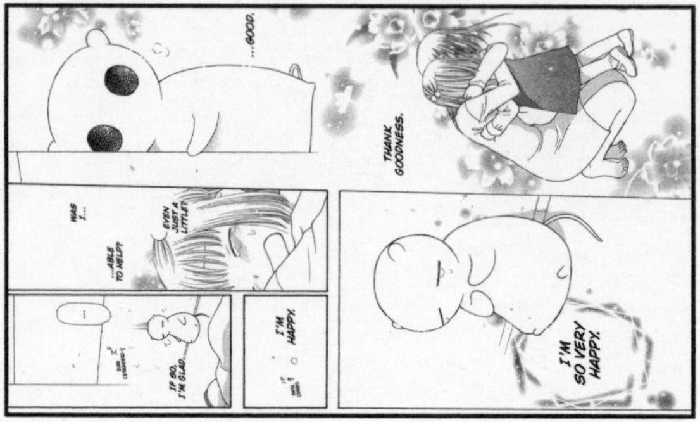

...GOOD.
THANK GOODNESS.
WAS I...
...ABLE TO HELP?
EVEN JUST A LITTLE?
...
IF SO, I'M GLAD.
I'M HAPPY.
I'M SO VERY HAPPY.

That same day

(119) (120) — Kyo promises Kyoko that he'll find Tohru. However, Yuki helps her first. Kyo stops going to see Kyoko after this.

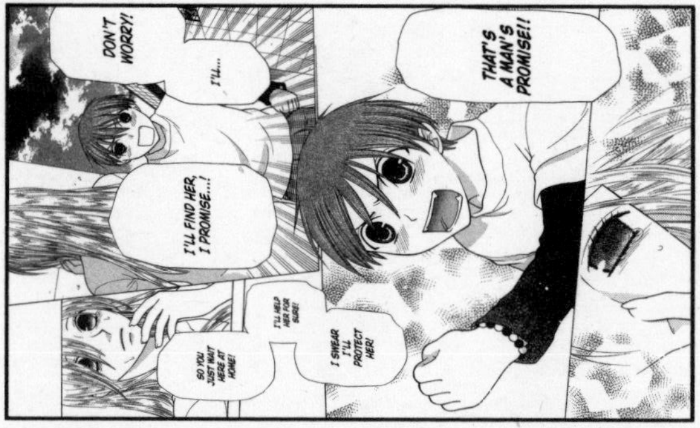

DON'T WORRY!
I'LL...
I'LL FIND HER, I PROMISE...!
THAT'S A MAN'S PROMISE!!
SO YOU JUST WAIT HERE AT HOME!
I'LL HELP HER FOR SURE!
I SWEAR I'LL PROTECT HER!

(14) — Hatsuharu talks to Yuki for the first time.

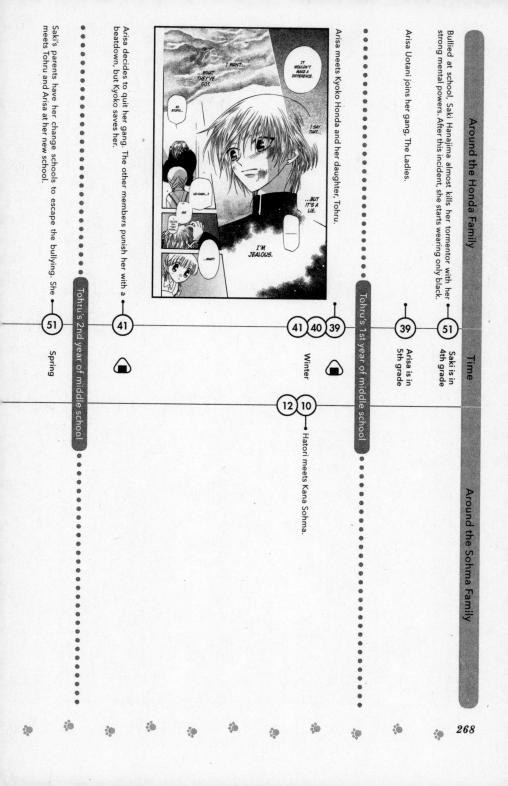

Around the Honda Family		Time		Around the Sohma Family
Bullied at school, Saki Hanajima almost kills her tormentor with her strong mental powers. After this incident, she starts wearing only black.	51	Saki is in 4th grade		
Arisa Uotani joins her gang, The Ladies.	39	Arisa is in 5th grade		
Tohru's 1st year of middle school				
Arisa meets Kyoko Honda and her daughter, Tohru.	39 40 41	Winter	10 12	Hatori meets Kana Sohma.
Arisa decides to quit her gang. The other members punish her with a beatdown, but Kyoko saves her.	41			
Tohru's 2nd year of middle school				
Saki's parents have her change schools to escape the bullying. She meets Tohru and Arisa at her new school.	51	Spring		

IT WOULDN'T MAKE A DIFFERENCE.
I SAY THAT...
...BUT IT'S A LIE.
I'M JEALOUS.
I WANT...
...WHAT THEY'VE GOT.
SO STUPID...
UO-CHAN...?
...WHAT?
AH
I CALLED YOU THAT AGAIN.

Fall–Winter

10 12 Hatori asks Akito for permission to marry Kana, but this provokes Akito's wrath, and the engagement is called off. This is when Hatori loses most of the sight in one eye, and he buries Kana's memories.

Winter

56

51 Tohru and Arisa learn Saki has powers, but they still accept her.

I...
...WANT TO BE TOGETHER ...
THAT'S ALL THERE IS TO IT...
I WANT TO STAY WITH YOU...

I'M SO...
...SORRY ...
...I COULDN'T ...
... PROTECT YOU.
I'M SORRY.
......
SORRY ...
I'M SORRY...
...HATORI ......
MEETING YOU...

101 Shigure sleeps with Ren. It's said that his punishment for this is being exiled from the Sohma compound.

Tohru's 1st year of high school

Beginning of the 1st year of high school

4 69 117 Yuki moves in with Shigure so he can attend high school nearby. Actually, Hatsuharu asked Shigure to rescue Yuki from the main house.

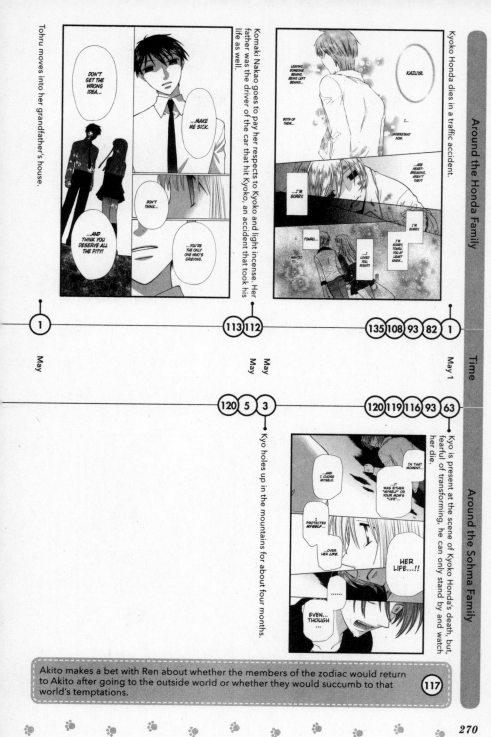

Around the Honda Family	Time	Around the Sohma Family
(1) (82) (93) (108) (135) Kyoko Honda dies in a traffic accident.	May 1	(63) (93) (116) (119) (120) Kyo is present at the scene of Kyoko Honda's death, but, fearful of transforming, he can only stand by and watch her die.
(112) (113) Komaki Nakao goes to pay her respects to Kyoko and light incense. Her father was the driver of the car that hit Kyoko, an accident that took his life as well.	May / May	(3) (5) (120) Kyo holes up in the mountains for about four months.
(1) Tohru moves into her grandfather's house.	May	

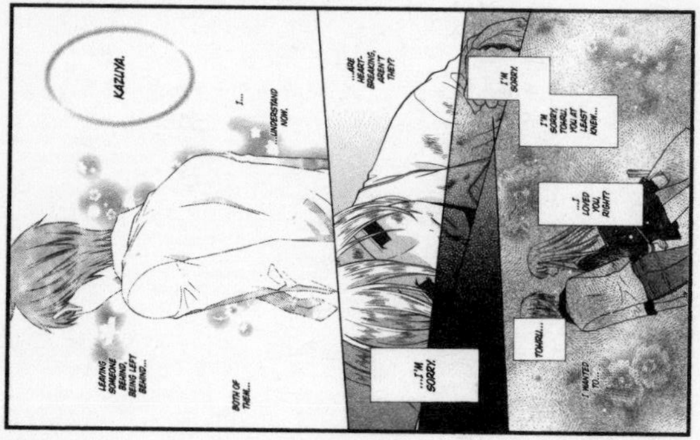
KAZUYA.
LEAVING SOMEONE BEHIND, BEING LEFT BEHIND...
BOTH OF THEM...
I...
...UNDERSTAND NOW.
...ARE HEART-BREAKING, AREN'T THEY?
...I'M SORRY.
I'M SORRY.
I'M SORRY, TOHRU. YOU AT LEAST KNEW...
TOHRU...
...I LOVED YOU, RIGHT?
I WANTED TO...

IN THAT MOMENT...
...IT WAS EITHER "MYSELF" OR YOUR MOM'S "LIFE"...
...AND I CHOSE MYSELF.
I PROTECTED MYSELF...
...OVER HER LIFE.
HER LIFE...!!
......
EVEN... THOUGH ...

...MAKE ME SICK.
DON'T THINK...
...YOU'RE THE ONLY ONE WHO'S GRIEVING.
DON'T GET THE WRONG IDEA...
...AND THINK YOU DESERVE ALL THE PITY!

Akito makes a bet with Ren about whether the members of the zodiac would return to Akito after going to the outside world or whether they would succumb to that world's temptations. (117)

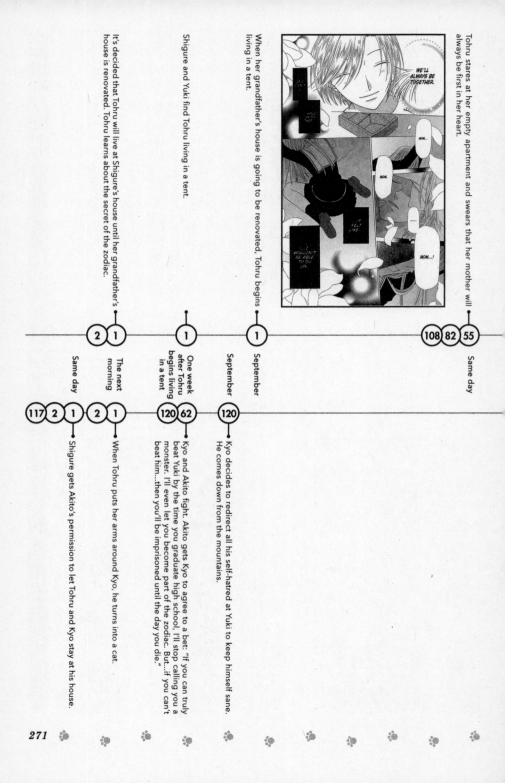

(55)(82)(108) Same day — Tohru stares at her empty apartment and swears that her mother will always be first in her heart.

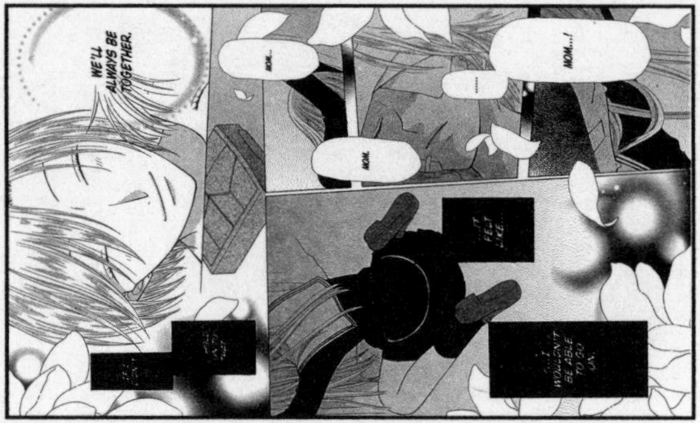
WE'LL ALWAYS BE TOGETHER.
MOM...
MOM.
......
MOM...!
...IT FELT LIKE...
...I WOULDN'T BE ABLE TO GO ON.

(1) September — When her grandfather's house is going to be renovated, Tohru begins living in a tent.

(120) September — Kyo decides to redirect all his self-hatred at Yuki to keep himself sane. He comes down from the mountains.

(1) One week after Tohru begins living in a tent — Shigure and Yuki find Tohru living in a tent.

(62)(120) One week after Tohru begins living in a tent — Kyo and Akito fight. Akito gets Kyo to agree to a bet: "If you can truly beat Yuki by the time you graduate high school, I'll stop calling you a monster. I'll even let you become part of the zodiac. But...if you can't beat him...then you'll be imprisoned until the day you die."

(1)(2) The next morning — It's decided that Tohru will live at Shigure's house until her grandfather's house is renovated. Tohru learns about the secret of the zodiac.

(1)(2) The next morning — When Tohru puts her arms around Kyo, he turns into a cat.

(1)(2)(117) Same day — Shigure gets Akito's permission to let Tohru and Kyo stay at his house.

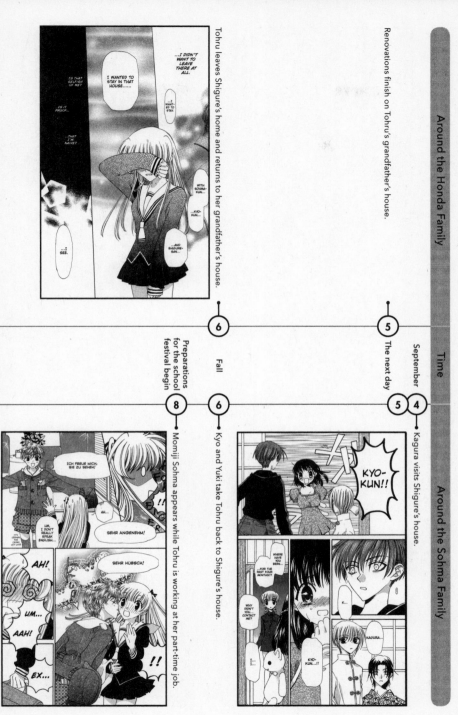

Around the Honda Family	Time	Around the Sohma Family
	September (4)	Kagura visits Shigure's house.
Renovations finish on Tohru's grandfather's house.	(5) The next day (5)	
Tohru leaves Shigure's home and returns to her grandfather's house.	(6) Fall (6)	Kyo and Yuki take Tohru back to Shigure's house.
	Preparations for the school festival begin (8)	Momiji Sohma appears while Tohru is working at her part-time job.

KYO-KUN!!
K...
KAGURA...
KYO-KUN...!!
WHERE HAVE YOU BEEN...
...FOR THE PAST FOUR MONTHS!?
WHY DIDN'T YOU... CONTACT ME?
I... I...

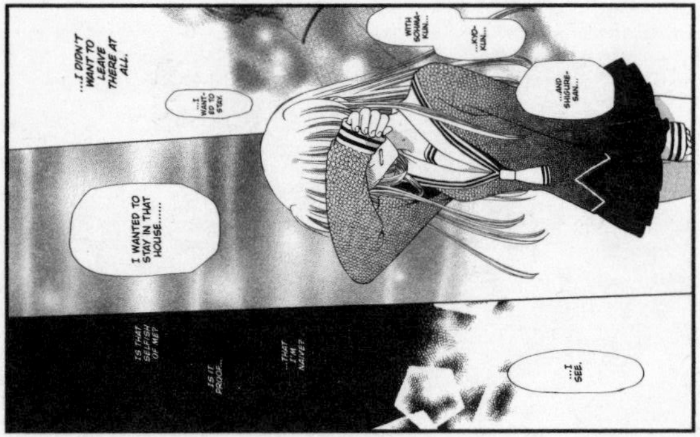
...I DIDN'T WANT TO LEAVE THERE AT ALL.
I WANTED TO STAY IN THAT HOUSE......
...I WANTED TO STAY.
WITH SOHMA-KUN...
...KYO-KUN...
...AND SHIGURE-SAN...
IS THAT SELFISH OF ME?
IS IT PROOF...
...THAT I'M NAIVE?
...I SEE.

ICH FREUE MICH, SIE ZU SEHEN!
AH...
UM, I DON'T REALLY SPEAK ENGLISH...
SEHR ANGENEHM!
SEHR HÜBSCH!
!!
AH!
UM...
AAH!
EX...

9 School festival

The school festival arrives. Class 1-D runs a rice ball stand.

DOES THE TASTINESS OF A RICE BALL HAVE ANYTHING TO DO WITH HOW IT'S ROLLED!?
THE RICE BALLS YOU MADE ARE REALLY GOOD, HONDA-SAN.
HUH!?
O-OH, I DIDN'T...
AND THE CAT RICE BALLS ARE CUTE! ♡
THANK YOU...
ACTUALLY, I THOUGHT OF MAKING RAT RICE BALLS TOO, BUT...
EWW, THAT'D BE GROSS... I WOULDN'T EAT THAT...
CANNIBALISM ...?
BUT...
...THE ONE WHO CONTRIBUTED MOST TO OUR CLASS'S SALES IS—
HEY!!
NOBODY SAID YOU COULD TAKE A PHOTO!!

Momiji Sohma and Hatori Sohma attend the festival. Hatori forcefully requests Tohru visit him at the Sohma compound on her next day off.

I WONDER WHAT IT IS...
WHA—?
HUH!? ME!?
WHO WOULD'VE THOUGHT I'D EVER MEET SOMEONE WHO COULD DO SOMETHING SO INCREDIBLE?
HEY.
UM, S-SEE YOU LATER.
THE ONE WHO ERASED THEIR MEMORIES...
I APOLOGIZE FOR CALLING YOU DOWN HERE.
I DIDN'T THINK I COULD GET A WORD IN WITH YUKI AROUND, LET ALONE KYO.
LESS THAN TWO MINUTES SINCE I WAS WARNED, AND I'M ALREADY ALONE WITH HIM—!!
HUH!?
THIS IS MY ADDRESS.
COME FOR A VISIT ON YOUR NEXT DAY OFF.

10 Her next day off

Tohru follows Hatori's instructions and visits him at the Sohma compound, where she learns about Kana.

I RECOMMEND...
...YOU LEAVE THAT HOUSE...
...AND HAVE NOTHING MORE TO DO WITH THE SOHMA FAMILY.
WHAT ......?
SHIGURE BEING WHO HE IS, I'M SURE HE LEFT YOU IN THE DARK.
YOU SEE, THE SOHMA FAMILY CONTINUES TO BE POSSESSED BY VENGEFUL SPIRITS. WE'RE NOT THE JOLLY BUNCH YOU PROBABLY IMAGINE.
WE ARE BIZARRE...
...DEVIOUS...
...AND CURSED.

Akito spots Tohru from her bedroom window.

11 New Year's

Yuki and Kyo skip the Sohma New Year's gathering for Tohru's sake.

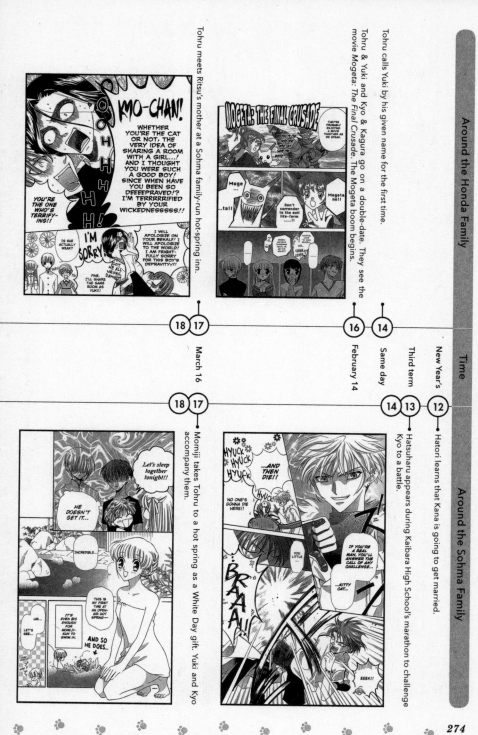

Around the Honda Family		Time		Around the Sohma Family
		New Year's	12	Hatori learns that Kana is going to get married.
		Third term	13	Hatsuharu appears during Kaibara High School's marathon to challenge Kyo to a battle.
Tohru calls Yuki by his given name for the first time.	14	Same day	14	
Tohru & Yuki and Kyo & Kagura go on a double-date. They see the movie *Mogeta: The Final Crusade*. The Mogeta boom begins.	16	February 14		
Tohru meets Ritsu's mother at a Sohma family-run hot-spring inn.	17 18	March 16	17 18	Momiji takes Tohru to a hot spring as a White Day gift. Yuki and Kyo accompany them.

MOGETA: THE FINAL CRUSADE
THEY'RE PROBABLY ENJOYING A MOVIE TOGETHER AS WE SPEAK.
Mogeta no!!
Moge ...
...ta!!
Don't surrender to the evil life-form ......!!

KYO-CHAN!
OOHHHHHH!
WHETHER YOU'RE THE CAT OR NOT, THE VERY IDEA OF SHARING A ROOM WITH A GIRL...! AND I THOUGHT YOU WERE SUCH A GOOD BOY! SINCE WHEN HAVE YOU BEEN SO DEEEEPRAVED!? I'M TERRRRRIFIED BY YOUR WICKEDNESSSSS!!
YOU'RE THE ONE WHO'S TERRIFY-ING!!
I WILL APOLOGIZE ON YOUR BEHALF! I WILL APOLOGIZE TO THE WORLD! I AM FRIGHT-FULLY SORRY FOR THIS BOY'S DEPRAVITYYY!
I'M SORRY!
IS SHE ACTUALLY WEAK?
FINE, I'LL SHARE THE SAME ROOM AS YUKI!!

IF YOU'RE A REAL MAN, YOU'LL ANSWER THE CALL OF ANY CHALLENGE...
...KITTY CAT...
YOU LITTLE ...
BRAAA!!
HYUCK HYUCK HYUCK
...AND THEN DIE!!
HYUCK!
NO ONE'S GONNA DIE HERE!!
EEEK!!

Let's sleep together tonight!!
HE DOESN'T GET IT...
INCREDIBLE...
THIS IS MY FIRST TIME AT AN OPEN-AIR HOT SPRING—
IT'S EVEN BIG ENOUGH FOR MOMIJI-KUN TO SWIM IN.
AND SO HE DOES...
UM...
LET'S SEE...

Tohru's 2nd year of high school

Entrance ceremony

(19) Akito shows up at the entrance ceremony and speaks to Tohru for the first time. (20)

(19) Momiji and Hatsuharu start attending Kaibara High School.

I-I DIDN'T EXPECT HIM TO BE SO...
...GENTLE.
I REALLY HOPE WE CAN BE FRIENDS.
AND PLEASE CONTINUE TAKING GOOD CARE...
...OF YUKI AND THE OTHERS.
AKITO...
AH...

Days after the entrance ceremony

(21) Ayame visits Shigure's house and takes Tohru out to lunch.

AND YET HE SEEMS TO BE IN HIGH SPIRITS.
TO BE HONEST, IT WAS A LET-DOWN.
YOU SEE, IF HE WAS VULNERABLE, I COULD HAVE PLAYED MY ROLE AS BIG BROTHER.
DO YOU... HAVE REGRETS?
ABOUT ...
... CREATING THAT RIFT...
......
IT'S STRANGE ...
...BUT AS YOU GET OLDER, THINGS YOU COULDN'T COMPREHEND IN CHILDHOOD...
...BECOME CLEAR.

May 1

(24) The first anniversary of Kyoko Honda's death. Tohru, Kyo, Yuki, Arisa, and Saki visit her grave.

NAH, NOTHIN'.
HE'S FINE...
REALLY?
AH!
THEN BOTH OF YOU COME OVER HERE.
HUH?
WE'RE READY.
YOU CAN'T HAVE A PICNIC IN FRONT OF A GRAVE—!!!
HUH?
IT'S FINE. BESIDES, KYOKO-SAN WOULD WANT US TO BE LOUD AND CHEERFUL.
WHAT IF SOMEBODY WHO WORKS HERE SEES US!?
THEN WE APOLOGIZE. DUUUH!

May 2

(25) (26) Shigure, Hatori, Kyo, and Yuki take Tohru to a Sohma vacation home.

May 3

(26) Ayame comes to the vacation home with photos of Kana's wedding ceremony.

(104) (38) Hiro tells Akito he's in love with Kisa. Angered, Akito seriously injures Kisa.

(27) Kisa starts middle school but stops talking after being bullied.

Around the Honda Family	Time		Around the Sohma Family
	Early Golden Week	27	Haru finds Kisa safe and sound (in tiger form) after she had run away.

...DON'T HATE ME.
TELL ME...
..."IT'S ALL RIGHT."

Around the Honda Family	Time		Around the Sohma Family
	May	28	Yuki agrees to become the president of the student council.
	Early June	31	Kazuma Sohma returns from his trip.
	Same night	32	Kyo's true form is revealed to Tohru.
		33	

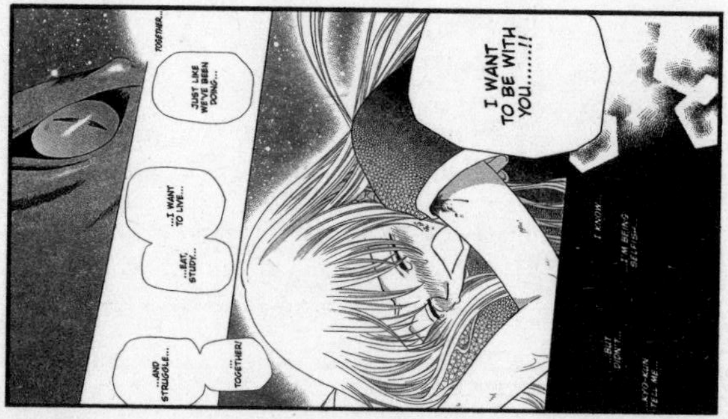
TOGETHER...
JUST LIKE WE'VE BEEN DOING...
...I WANT TO LIVE...
...EAT, STUDY...
...AND STRUGGLE...
... TOGETHER!
I WANT TO BE WITH YOU......!!
I KNOW...
...I'M BEING SELFISH...
...BUT DIDN'T...
...KYO-KUN TELL ME...

Before summer vacation

37 — Hiro comes to see Tohru.

TOOK YOU LONG ENOUGH, STUPID WOMAN!!
A SOHMA ...
ONE OF THE ZODIAC...!

104 79 78 38 — When Akito finds out Isuzu is dating Hatsuharu, she pushes Isuzu out a two-story window, which causes serious injuries.

Before summer vacation

43 — After Isuzu breaks up with Hatsuharu, he switches to Black Haru and destroys a classroom.

Same day

43 — Ritsu visits Shigure's home.

Before summer vacation

45 44

RICCHAN-SAN!?
!?
......!?
AAAAAAH! EVEN A STRANGER KNOWS MY NAAAME!
U-UM...
I'VE BEEN LIVING CAREFREE ALL THIS TIME, UTTERLY IGNORANT OF THE FACT THAT MY NAME IS NOTORIOUS! I'M SORRY! AND I'M SORRY TO THOSE WHO HAVE THE UNFORTUNATE BURDEN OF SHARING THE SAME NAME AS ME!
I'M SOOORRYYYY!

50 46 — Arisa meets Kureno at the convenience store where she works.

AH!
I THANK YOU FOR YOUR KINDNESS...
NO PROBLEM... BUT THAT'S KINDA DANGEROUS.
YOU SHOULD USE A BASKET...
A BASKET?
OH. OH YES, I SHOULD HAVE USED ONE.
AWW...
......
AH HA HA!!
NOW I'VE DONE IT...
HA!

Around the Honda Family	Time	Around the Sohma Family
	Summer vacation (49)	Yuki meets Kakeru Manabe and Machi Kuragi.
Arisa meets Kureno Sohma again. (50)	Summer vacation	
Yuki asks Tohru about the baseball cap she has in her room. (53)	Summer vacation (53)	Momiji invites Tohru and the others to go on a trip.
	Same day (53) (78)	Isuzu visits Shigure to ask him about breaking the curse.
	The next day (54) (55) (57) ~ (65)	To beat the summer heat, they go on a trip to a Sohma vacation home.

I have no idea who he was...
I don't even remember what he looked like...
My memory is fuzzy...
Then why did you keep it all these years...? It's all beat-up...
Because it's a precious memory.
Because I was so happy...
...when he...
...saved me.

I'm black, by the way!!
You're... black...?
Coffee? Race?
This is an absolute!! It's the one thing I'm not backing down on!!
Otherwise, I'm looking forward to working with you!!
What?
Well...
I said everything I wanted to say, and now I'm sleeeepy!!
Wait......
Would you at least tell me who you people are...!?
I already said—I'm Manabe—
That's not what I mean!!

...huh.
......?
That is... kind of amazing.
Honda-san's a better swimmer than I imagined...
...but it looks like she wasn't breathing.
What!!?
Wheeze
Wheeze
Wheeze
Wheeze

Summer vacation **56** — Hatori and Mayuko Shiraki meet again.

57

Summer vacation **58** — The gang learns Hiro's mother is pregnant.

Summer vacation **58** ~ Summer vacation **65** — Akito comes to the vacation home.

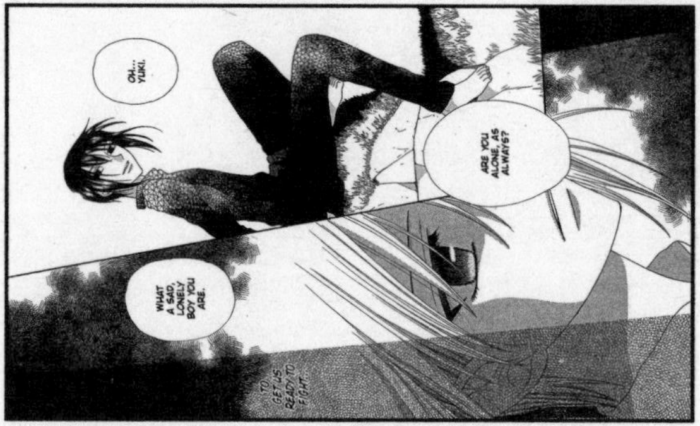
Oh... Yuki.
Are you alone, as always?
What a sad, lonely boy you are.
To get us ready to fight.

Summer vacation **61** — Isuzu Sohma appears at the vacation home.

Summer vacation **61** — Tohru learns that a famous priest created Kyo's beads hundreds of years ago. They're made from human bones coated with blood, and people's lives were sacrificed to make them.

The previous cat...
...was master-san's grand-father.
...did the previous cat...
...also wear those prayer beads...?
Yeah.
They're very... unusual, right?
I wonder what the beads are made from.
Human bones.
Wha ......?
From some famous monk or whatever...
Apparently, the red ones were coated with human blood.
We're talkin' hundreds of years ago though...

Around the Honda Family	Time	Around the Sohma Family
	Summer vacation (62) (63)	Kyo realizes he loves Tohru.
	Summer vacation (63)	Kyo learns Akito is trying to use Tohru for some unknown reason.
(65) Tohru learns that Akito is the god who controls the souls of the members of the zodiac.	Summer vacation (65)	Akito introduces Kureno to Tohru.

I LOVE YOU.
I LOVE YOU...
...JUST THE WAY YOU ARE.
I LOVE YOU SO MUCH.

OH... RIGHT.
I SHOULD INTRODUCE YOU.
THIS IS KURENO SOHMA.
...HE'S THE ROOSTER.
HUH ...?
NICE...
...TO MEET YOU.
...TOHRU-SAN.
HUH...AH, N-NICE TO... MEET YOU.
THE ROOSTER ...
THIS MAN...
...IS THE ROOSTER.

I AM THE ONE WHO CONTROLS THEM.
I AM THE MASTER OF THEIR SOULS.
...NOW YOU KNOW.

- **66** — First day of second term — Yuki meets Kimi Toudou and Naohito Sakuragi for the first time.
- **66, 67** — Same day — Tohru visits Kazuma to ask him the truth about Kyo's imprisonment and to find a way to break the curse. She learns that the bond itself is the curse.
- **68** — A Sunday in September — Kagura tries to make peace with her feelings for Kyo.
- **69, 70** — The next day — Yuki learns that he was only released from Akito's captivity because Hatsuharu begged for Shigure's help.
- **71** — Parent-teacher conference — Saki falls in love at first sight with Kazuma Sohma.
- **76, 77** — Class trip — Tohru's class goes to Kyoto for the school trip.
- **77** — Class trip — Saki says she saw Tohru and Kakeru together once some time ago.
- **80** — Tohru learns that Isuzu is also trying to break the curse.
- **78, 79, 80** — When Isuzu collapses at Shigure's home, Tohru helps her.

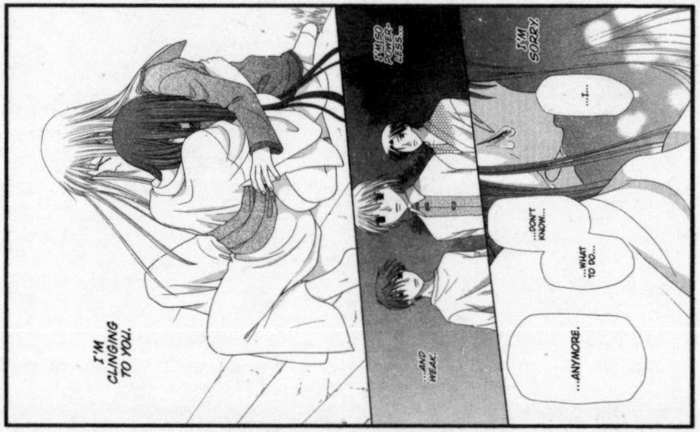
I'M CLINGING TO YOU.
I'M SO POWERLESS...
...AND WEAK.
I'M SORRY.
...I...
...DON'T KNOW...
...WHAT TO DO...
...ANYMORE.

- **82** — Tohru suggests to Isuzu that they ask Kureno about the curse, but Isuzu shoots down the idea. Isuzu doesn't think of Kureno as a member of the zodiac, let alone trust him.

Around the Honda Family		Time		Around the Sohma Family
The class puts on a play, "Cinderella-ish." Tohru plays the mean stepsister, Saki is Cinderella, and Arisa plays the prince's friend.	87 88 89	Festival	87 88 89	For the class's play, "Cinderella-ish," Kyo plays the prince, and Yuki is the fairy godmother.
		Third term	96 97 98 101	Kureno confesses (separately) to Shigure and Tohru that he's been freed from the curse. He also reveals to Tohru that Akito is a woman.
			106 115	Prompted by Ren, Isuzu tries to steal the small box from Akito's room, but Akito finds her. Shigure is the one who told Ren about the box's existence.

YOU'RE TELLING ME YOU HAVE THE CHANCE TO SEE HER AGAIN, AND YOU'RE JUST GONNA THROW IT AWAY!?
AND YOU CALL YOURSELF A MAN!?
HEY...
THINK ABOUT ALL THE PEOPLE WHO WANT TO SEE SOMEONE SO BADLY, BUT THEY JUST CAN'T!!
THEY WANT TO MEET...
THEY WANT TO SEE HIM...!
COME AND SEE ME, DAMMIT!!!
Though his friend's persuasion was colored by personal feelings, the prince was swayed.
...WHO?
...
That's right...He realized something important.

SO I'M NO LONGER...
...A MEMBER OF THE ZODIAC.
HE HARDLY EVEN COUNTS AS ONE OF US ZODIAC MEMBERS.
I CAN'T...
IT HAPPENED YEARS AGO.
I WAS A LITTLE YOUNGER THAN YOU ARE NOW.
...BEEN BROKEN.

Tohru's 3rd year of high school

Around the Honda Family		Time		Around the Sohma Family
		April	104	Kureno frees Isuzu from the isolation room (meant for the Cat), where Akito had imprisoned her upon finding her trying to steal the box.
Tohru learns the curse will break—eventually.	107	April	107	Shigure tells Isuzu the curse will eventually break on its own, even if they don't do anything.
Tohru remembers when she met Kakeru and Komaki before.	112	The beginning of summer		

Before summer vacation — 115 116 — Momiji is freed from the curse.

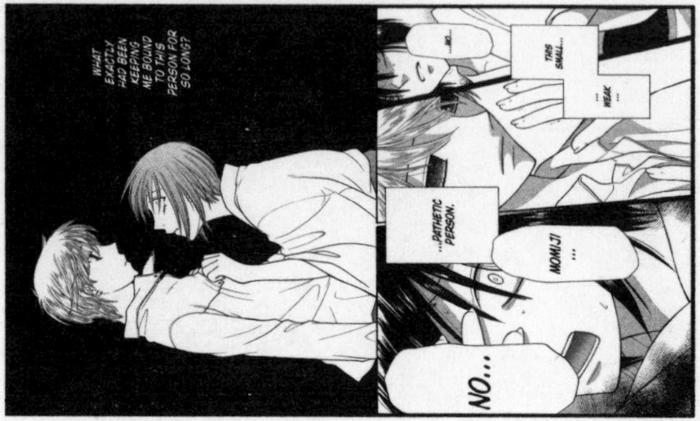

WHAT EXACTLY HAD BEEN KEEPING ME BOUND TO THIS PERSON FOR SO LONG?
...NO...
THIS SMALL...
...WEAK...
...PATHETIC PERSON.
MOMIJI...
NO...

Before summer vacation — 118 — Hiro is freed from the curse.

Same day — 118 — Akito stabs Kureno and runs away from the Sohma compound.

Same day — 119 — Kyo confesses to Tohru that he was at the scene of Kyoko's accident and just stood by when she was killed.

YOUR MOTHER...
...WAS LYING IN A POOL OF BLOOD.
SHE NOTICED ME STANDING THERE.
SHE TOLD ME...
..."I'LL NEVER FORGIVE YOU"...
THAT'S WHAT...
...IT SOUNDED LIKE, AT LEAST...
I'LL NEVER FORGIVE YOU...

119 120 — Tohru confesses her feelings to Kyo but is rebuffed.

BE-CAUSE!
NO MATTER WHAT...
...I CAN'T STOP MYSELF...
...FROM FEELING THIS WAY ABOUT YOU...
IS THAT WRONG...!?

Around the Honda Family	Time	Around the Sohma Family
Tohru asks Akito if they can be friends.	(121) Tohru is hospitalized	
	(124) A short while afterward	Akito visits Kureno and Tohru in the hospital.
	(126) 🍙	Kyo visits his father and realizes his mother did not commit suicide because of him but because of his father's verbal abuse.
	(126) Same day	Akito decides to demolish the Cat's isolation room. Kyo decides to live free from that day forth.
	(127) A short while afterward	Kureno leaves the Sohma compound without telling anyone where he's going.
	(129) Tohru is released from the hospital	Kyo confesses his feelings to Tohru.
	(129)(130) Same day	Kyo is released from the curse.

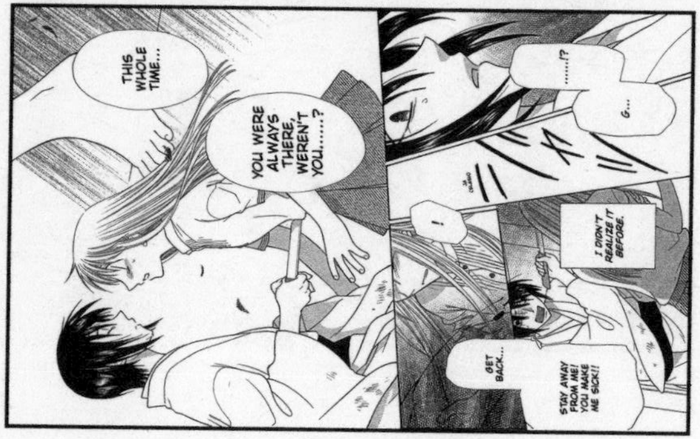
THIS WHOLE TIME...
YOU WERE ALWAYS THERE, WEREN'T YOU......?
......!?
G...
!
I DIDN'T REALIZE IT BEFORE.
GET BACK...
STAY AWAY FROM ME! YOU MAKE ME SICK!!

IF I'VE GOT...
...A LIFE AHEAD OF ME...
...I WANT TO SHARE IT WITH YOU.
...BE WITH YOU...!
I DON'T WANT ANYBODY ELSE.

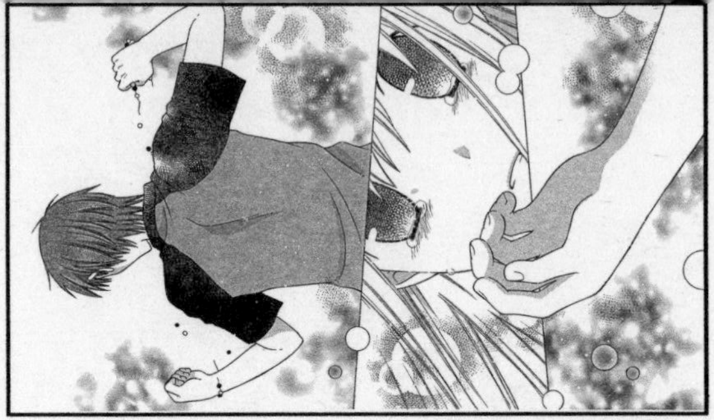

Same day (130)(131) • Ayame, Ritsu, Kisa, Kagura, Isuzu, Hatsuharu, Hatori, and Shigure are released from the curse. Last but not least, Yuki is also released from the curse.

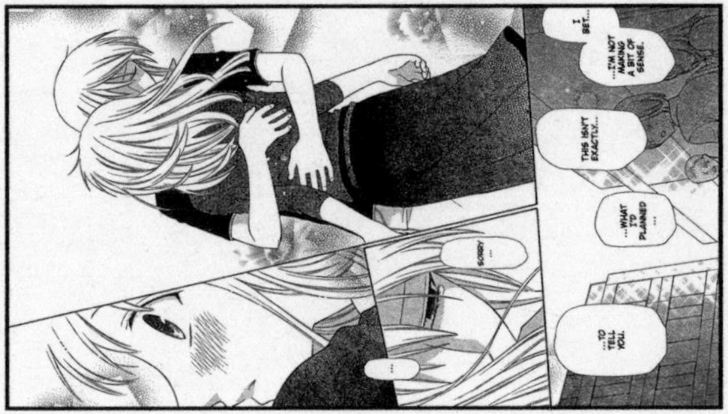

I BET...
...I'M NOT MAKING A BIT OF SENSE.
THIS ISN'T EXACTLY...
...WHAT I'D PLANNED...
SORRY...
...TO TELL YOU.
...

(132) • Shigure's schemes have paid off. He has Akito all to himself at last.

(134) • Kyo asks Tohru to come with him after they graduate high school.

(135)

Summer vacation (135) • Tohru agrees to Kyo's wish.

After graduation (136) • Tohru and Kyo embark on their new life together.

Lovey-dovey years begin

FRUITS BASKET SERIALIZATION HISTORY

Many readers supported this series through the eight years and four months of serialization. Let's take a look back at *Furuba*'s journey in *Hana-Yume* as well as the old covers and color opening-page artwork.

LEGEND

1998...Year of publication

Issue 15 ...Issue of *Hana to Yume*

Cover...Cover illustration

Chapter 1...Chapter number

Color opening spread...2-page illustrated spread in color at the front of the magazine

Color spread...2-page illustrated spread in color

Color opening page...1-page illustration in color at the front of the magazine

Dining Table...Sohma family dining table

Front...Frontispiece

P...Prize/Present

Bonus...Bonus included

All...Something free for everyone

※Note: Some of the names of the projects have been shortened.

お待たせ♥ピッカピカ新連載46P
フルーツバスケット
高屋奈月

▶ Fruits Basket Chapter 1 color opening page

16
46P
フルーツバスケット
高屋奈月

◀ Hana to Yume Issue 16, 1998 cover

1998 — Issue 15

Preview of the new series
1 page

Issue 16

Cover
Chapter 1
Color opening page + 46 pages
Front, P: Peel-off silver prize
Bonus: Summer vacation notebook

Issue 17

Chapter 2
30 pages

Issue 18

Chapter 3
30 pages

Bonus: *Quiz Book*

Issue 19

Chapter 4
30 pages

P: *Hana-Yume* boys' interior goods (aroma photo stand)

Issue 20

Chapter 5
Color opening page + 30 pages
P: Big postcard and telephone card

Issue 21

Chapter 6
30 pages

フルーツバスケット
高屋奈月

▶ Fruits Basket Chapter 5 color opening page

花とゆめCOMICS
フルーツバスケット
高屋奈月 1

Hana to Yume Comics
Volume 1
Published January 1999

MMPH?

大人気ありがとう♥連載再開33P
十二支へんしんホームコメディ 第7話
フルーツバスケット
高屋奈月

▶ *Fruits Basket* Chapter 7 color opening page

フルーツバスケット

◀ *Hana to Yume* Issue 23, 1998 cover

1998 — Issue 22

Announcement of the series' return
1 page
P: Happy Cooking (Tohru apron)

Issue 23

Cover
Chapter 7
Color opening page + 32 pages
P: Original panel clock

Issue 24

Chapter 8
30 pages

P: Original Christmas item (tote bag)

1999 — Issue 1

Chapter 9
30 pages

P: All-Star autographed New Year's card
Bonus: All-Star calendar

← **All**: 99 Dream² telephone card

Issue 2

Chapter 10
30 pages

P: All-Star favorite item (autographed illustrated rough sketch)

Issue 3

Chapter 11
Color opening spread + 30 pages

Issue 4

Chapter 12
30 pages

Issue 5

Announcement of the series' return
1 page
Bonus: Colorful B5 (7.17" × 10.12") file folder

All: 99 Dream² telephone card ←

WELCOME 1999
フルーツバスケット

▶ *Fruits Basket* Chapter 11 color opening spread

花とゆめCOMICS
フルーツバスケット
高屋奈月
2

Hana to Yume Comics
Volume 2
Published June 1999

STILL
DREAMING

フルーツバスケット
高屋奈月

▲ *Fruits Basket* Chapter 13 color opening page

8
新学期フェスタ♥スタート
フルーツバスケット
高屋奈月

▲ *Hana to Yume* Issue 8, 1999 cover

絶・好・調!!
第16回
フルーツバスケット
高屋奈月
NATSUKI TAKAYA

▲ *Fruits Basket* Chapter 16 color opening page

1999

Issue 6

Chapter 13
Color opening page +
30 pages
Front: Love psychology chart
P: Lunchbox and pouch

Issue 7

Chapter 14
30 pages

Issue 8

Cover
Chapter 15
30 pages

Issue 9

Chapter 16
Color opening page +
30 pages

← **All**: Exciting stationery set

Issue 10

Chapter 17
30 pages

P: *Hana-Yume* Stars triple stamp
Bonus: CD bag

All: Exciting stationery set ←

Issue 11

Chapter 18
30 pages

P: Autographed fancy illustrated telephone card / *Hana to Yume* 25th-anniversary clock

Issue 12

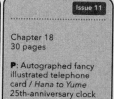

P: Waiting for Summer ★ Music (Tohru headphone stereo)

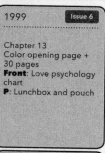

花とゆめCOMICS
フルーツバスケット
高屋奈月 3

Hana to Yume Comics
Volume 3
Published September 1999

MMM...

16

▲ *Hana to Yume Issue 16, 1999 cover*

さらにWAKU'十二支コメディ
フルーツバスケット
[第19回]
連載再開!
32P
入学&進級祝
巻頭カラー
高屋奈月
NEWS

▲ *Fruits Basket Chapter 19 color opening spread*

1999

Issue 13

Chapter 19
Color opening spread + 30 pages
Front, **P**: Silver peel-off prize, "Kyo's K1 ★ Revenge!"
P: Lunchtime goods (mug cup)

Issue 14

Chapter 20
30 pages

P: *Hana-Yume* character's image fragrance (Tohru handbag)

Issue 15

Chapter 21
30 pages

Issue 16

Cover
Chapter 22
30 pages

P: Let's Go to *Hana-Yume*'s Summer Fest 25! (shoulder bag)
Bonus: Tote bag

Issue 17

Chapter 23
Color opening page + 30 pages
Bonus: Special character card

Issue 18

Chapter 24
30 pages

Issue 19

Side story
4 page

← **All**: *Special CD Set*

ラブリー超人気!!
フルーツバスケット
高屋奈月

▲ *Fruits Basket Chapter 23 color opening page*

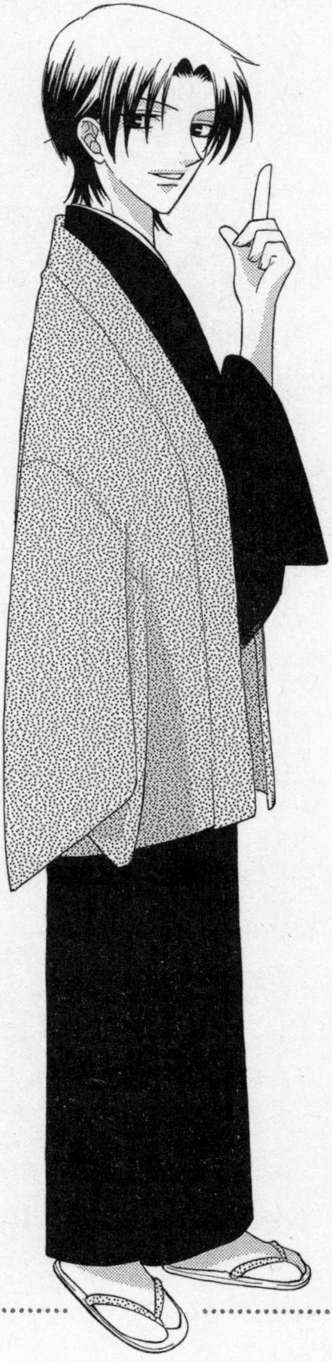

花とゆめCOMICS
フルーツバスケット
高屋奈月 4

Hana to Yume Comics
Volume 4
Published January 2000

IT TAKES A LONG TIME FOR HIM TO GET UP...

人形のようにかわいい杞紗――
でも心まで人形のようにならないで
フルーツバスケット
高屋奈月

▼ *Fruits Basket* Chapter 28 color opening page

大人気連載再開♥
いよいよラストチャンス!!
フルーツバスケット
高屋奈月

▼ *Fruits Basket* Chapter 25 color title-page spread

1999

Issue 20

Chapter 25
Color opening spread +
30 pages

All: *Special CD Set*

Issue 21

Chapter 26
30 pages

Issue 22

Chapter 27
30 pages

P: Work item you long for (Shigure's photo stand with light attached)

Issue 23

Chapter 28
Color opening page +
30 pages
P: *Hana-Yume* Super Premium Collection part 3 *Fruits Basket*

Issue 24

Chapter 29
Color opening page +
30 pages

2000

Issue 1

Chapter 30
30 pages

P: *Hana-Yume* All-Star ★ autographed New Year's card
Bonus: 2000 calendar

Issue 2

Front: 2000 ★ Heart-throbbing compatibility diagnosis
P: Monopolize a character ♥ item (Yuki magazine case)

十二支ホームコメディ
フルーツバスケット
【第29回】
高屋奈月

▼ *Fruits Basket* Chapter 29 color opening page

花とゆめCOMICS
フルーツバスケット
高屋奈月
5

Hana to Yume Comics
Volume 5
Published April 2000

NYAH...

フルーツバスケット
十二支だけで行われる
年越しの夜の宴
旧年の者から新年の者へ
年に一度だけの、神聖なる祝いの舞い…

▶ Fruits Basket Chapter 32 color opening spread

3
フルーツバスケット
ミレニアム★スターズ
テレホンカード

▶ Hana to Yume Issue 3, 2000 cover

2000

Issue 3

Cover
Chapter 31
30 pages

Bonus: Double notebook with horoscopes attached

Issue 4

Chapter 32
Color opening spread + 30 pages
Front: Character-contest solicitation

Issue 5

Chapter 33
30 pages

Issue 6

Chapter 34
30 pages

All: Millennium★ Stars telephone card

Issue 7

Chapter 35
Color opening page + 30 pages
P: Exciting Spring Music♪ (portable CD case)

Issue 8

Chapter 36
Color opening page + 30 pages
Front: Character-contest results

Issue 9

P: Quiz & original clock (panel clock)

フルーツバスケット
高屋奈月

▶ Fruits Basket Chapter 36 title page

フルーツバスケット
高屋奈月

▶ Fruits Basket Chapter 35 title page

花とゆめCOMICS
フルーツバスケット
高屋奈月 6

Hana to Yume Comics
Volume 6
Published August 2000

Guten Morgen!

11
270YEN
フルーツバスケット
高屋奈月

▲ *Hana to Yume* Issue 11, 2000 cover

本日も晴天なり。
気分爽快！
連載再開
十二支ホームコメディ★第37回
フルーツバスケット
高屋奈月
NATSUKI TAKAYA

▲ *Fruits Basket* Chapter 37 color opening spread

2000

Issue 10
Chapter 37
Color opening spread + 30 pages

Issue 11
Cover
Chapter 38
30 pages
P: *Hana-Yume* All-Star ★ heart-shaped ♥ signed autograph board / quiz & present (Tohru net bag)
Bonus: Sticker set

Issue 12
Chapter 39
30 pages
P: *Hana-Yume* Stars ★ premium stamp

Issue 13
Chapter 40
30 pages

← **All**: 2000 special-secret ★ tapestry

Issue 14
Chapter 41
Color opening page + 30 pages
P: *Hana-Yume* character's image fragrance (Kagura potpourri photo frame)

Issue 15
Chapter 42
30 pages

Issue 16
Bonus: Clear file folder

All: 2000 special-secret ★ tapestry ←

第41回
高屋奈月
NATSUKI TAKAYA PRESENTS
フルーツバスケット

▲ *Fruits Basket* Chapter 41 color opening page

花とゆめCOMICS
フルーツバスケット
高屋奈月 7

Hana to Yume Comics
Volume 7
Published August 2001

DIDN'T GET ENOUGH SLEEP...

18
サマーフェア開催!!
フルーツバスケット
花ざかりの君たちへ

▶ *Hana to Yume* Issue 18, 2000 cover

元気いっぱい♥連載再開!!
フルーツバスケット

▶ *Fruits Basket* Chapter 43 color opening spread

2000 — Issue 17
Chapter 43
Color opening spread
30 pages

Issue 18
Cover
Chapter 44
30 pages

P: Reversible body pillow
Bonus: Double character ★ letter set

2000 — Issue 19 ~2001 — Issue 17
★ For details, see pp. 302–303

2001 — Issue 18
Announcement of the series' return
1 page

← **All**: 2000 official ★ trading card set (~Issue 20)

All: (Issue 17~) *Furuba* anniversary goods ←

Issue 19
Cover
Chapter 45
Color opening page + 31 pages
1-page greeting
P: Yuki & Kyo meal set

Issue 20
Chapter 46
Color opening spread + 30 pages

Dining table: 1 page

Issue 21
Chapter 47
30 pages

Issue 22
Chapter 48
30 pages

P: Fall-colored interior goods (Tohru anything message pod)

All: Exciting tranquility cushion

← **All**: 2002 happy ♥ system notepad

▼ *Fruits Basket* Chapter 46 color opening spread

TVアニメ毎週木曜日夕方6時より絶賛放送中!!
フルーツバスケット
高屋奈月

連載再開!!
みなさん お久しぶりなのですっ!
十二支ホームコメディ
第45回
フルーツバスケット
高屋奈月

▶ *Fruits Basket* Chapter 45 color opening page

19
フルバ再開!!
日高万里新連載!!
フルーツバスケット
高屋奈月
ひつじの涙
日高万里

▶ *Hana to Yume* Issue 19, 2001 cover

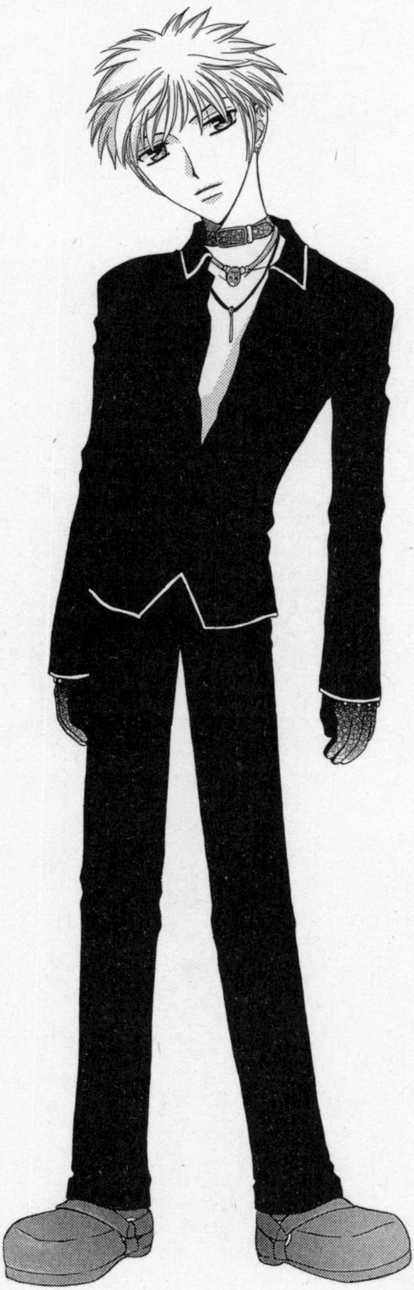

花とゆめCOMICS
フルーツバスケット
高屋奈月
8

Hana to Yume Comics
Volume 8
Published January 2002

FRUITS BASKET BOOKSHELF

Many *Furuba*-related publications such as art books, fan books, and calendars have also been released. There are so many memorable items tied to this series. Do you have any of them?

★Denotes out-of-print

HAKUSENSHA ENGLISH COMICS
フルーツバスケット
FRUITS BASKET
英語版

***Fruits Basket* Hakusensha English Comics**
(Published November 2003) ★
It's time to study with Chapters 1-3 of *Furuba* in English! ♪ Japanese lines also included in the sidebars. A5 size.

フルーツバスケット
高屋奈月
キャラクターブック

***Fruits Basket* Character Book**
by Natsuki Takaya
(Published July 2001) ★
Includes character introductions and an interview with Takaya-sensei. *Furuba's* first book. B5 size variation.

Wow,Kyo!
「すごいです、夾君!」
Fruitsbasket is out in English!!
「英語版「フルーツバスケット」が発売されるんだそうですよ!!」
Wouldn't it be great if readers learned English and had fun!
「お役に立てたら嬉しいですね!」
待て…
待て待ておまえっ
何言ってんだかわかんねーぞおいっ

▲Kyo: Wait... / Hold on a second. / I got no idea what the hell you're sayin'!

Hana to Yume Special
***Fruits Basket* Special**
(Published July 2001) ★
Summary of *Furuba*, published while the TV anime was on the air. Included Chapters 1-6 and eight pages drawn just for this book.
B5 size.

フルーツバスケット
すぺしゃる
TVアニメ絶賛放送中!!

Issue 24	Issue 23	Issue 22	Issue 21	Issue 20	2000 Issue 19
Dining table: 1 page	**Dining table**: 1 page **P**: *Hana-Yume* couples ★ illustrated item (vinyl feather cushion)	**Dining table**: 1 page **Bonus**: Zodiac playing cards	**Front**, **P**: Yuki & Kyo tea table	**Dining Table**: 2 pages **P**: Always Together exciting original item (bath clock)	Announcement about the hiatus 1 page

All: 2000 official ★ trading card set ←

Issue 6	Issue 5	Issue 4	Issue 3	Issue 2	2001 Issue 1
Front: All-Star illustrated contest		**Bonus**: Postcard set		*Furuba* learn-everything dictionary 12 pages **Front**, **P**: *Furuba* bathroom goods **Bonus**: Schedule book	**P**: *Hana-Yume* ★ All-Star autographed New Year's card (Ayame New Year's card case) **Bonus**: All-Star calendar

All: *Hana-Yume* All-Star telephone card

2001 FRUITS BASKET
Calendar

2001 *Fruits Basket* Calendar
(Released November 2000) ★
The first calendar was large-size and included stickers.

Illustrated by Natsuki Takaya
Fruits Basket
フルーツバスケット
高屋奈月

Fruits Basket* *Natsuki Takaya Art Book
(Published April 2004) ★
The first art book included illustrations from 1998 through 2002. There are comments for each illustration. A4 size.

2002 FRUITS BASKET 365 DAILY CALENDAR

2002 *Fruits Basket* Daily Pad Calendar
(Released in December 2001) ★
Daily pad calendar that had 365 lines of dialogue and illustrations.

花とゆめCOMICSスペシャル
フルーツバスケット
ファンブック〔猫〕高屋奈月

Fruits Basket Fan Book (Cat)
(Published May 2005)
The first official fan book is the same size as the original collected Japanese volumes. Shiny ★ stickers are on the front. Includes the *Sohma Family Diary* story drawn just for this book (paperback).

FRUITS BASKET

2003 *Fruits Basket* Tabletop Postcard Calendar
(Released in December 2002) ★
Tabletop calendar that included detachable postcards.

花とゆめCOMICSスペシャル
フルーツバスケット
ファンブック〔宴〕高屋奈月

Fruits Basket Fan Book (Banquet)
(Published March 2007)
The second official fan book, published to commemorate the completion of the series. Includes the *Sohma Family Festival* story drawn just for this book. Comes with mini art book (paperback).

Issue 12	Issue 11	Issue 10	Issue 9	Issue 8	Issue 7
Dining table: 1 page	TV anime event announcement 2 pages	**Front**: TV anime event participation solicitation **P**: *Hana-Yume* Stars triple stamp	**Dining table**: 1 page **Front**: TV anime version coming!	**Dining table**: 1 page	**Dining table**: 2 pages
All: Best secret key animation reproduction set					

Issue 17	Issue 16	Issue 15		Issue 14	Issue 13
P: All-original ★ summer zakka (rainproof, clear player)			Cover (anime illustration) **Front, P**: Yuki & Kyo cushion **Bonus**: Colorful memo pad	**Dining table**: 2 pages **P**: *Hana-Yume* character's image fragrance (Kyo dome-shaped clock)	**Dining table**: 1 page
← **All**: *Furuba* anniversary goods					

TVアニメも絶好調!!
十二支ホームコメディ!!
フルーツバスケット
第49回
十二支だけの新年の舞い
はとりから綾女へ
そして来年は…？
高屋奈月

▶ *Fruits Basket* Chapter 49 color spread

24
Xmasパーティー号
フルーツバスケット
高屋奈月

▶ *Hana to Yume* Issue 24, 2001 cover

2001 Issue 23	Issue 24	2002 Issue 1	Issue 2
Dining table: 1 page **Bonus**: Mini memo message set	Cover Chapter 49 Color spread + 30 pages	Chapter 50 30 pages **P**: All-Star autographed New Year's card **Bonus**: 2002 All-Star calendar	**Front**: *Hana-Yume* New Year's doll puppet show
All: 2002 happy ♥ system notepad		**All**: Plush stuffed ♥ Yuki & Kyo	

Issue 3	Issue 4	Issue 5	Issue 6
Chapter 51 Color opening page + 50 pages **Bonus**: 2002 *Hana-Yume* super sticker collection	Cover Chapter 52 30 pages **P**: Quiz & present (first-aid set) **Bonus**: Triple clear letter set	Chapter 53 30 pages **Front**: *Hana-Yume* ★ magical sweets recipe	
All: Dream star ★ telephone card			

4
フルーツバスケット高屋奈月

▶ *Hana to Yume* Issue 4, 2002 cover

フルーツバスケット
高屋奈月

▶ *Fruits Basket* Chapter 51 color opening page

JUST
WAKING
UP!

花とゆめCOMICS
フルーツバスケット
高屋奈月
9

Hana to Yume Comics
Volume 9
Published June 2002

どうして こんなにも 胸が しめつけられるのだろう…?
十二支ホームコメディ
フルーツバスケット
第54回
高屋奈月

▶ *Fruits Basket* Chapter 54 color opening spread

2002

Issue 7

Chapter 54
Color opening spread + 30 pages
P: Super original goods (clear desk pad / mini card set / clear postcard)

Issue 8

Chapter 55
30 pages

Issue 9

Chapter 56
30 pages

P: *Hana-Yume* ♪ after-school item (piggy bank)
Bonus: Postcard set

Issue 10

← **All**: Super-big ★ clear poster

Issue 11

Cover
Chapter 57
Color opening spread + 30 pages
Front: All *Hana-Yume* friends ♥ illustration contest results
P: *Hana-Yume* All ★ Star autographed cardboard

Issue 12

Chapter 58
30 pages

P: *Hana-Yume* all lovely character stamp

Issue 13

Chapter 59
30 pages

P: Colorful interior item (tapestry pocket)

All: Super-big ★ clear poster ←

Issue 14

P: Early-summer items (Shigure, Mayuko)
Bonus: Going-out bag

← **All**: Little character ★ fastener accessory

お日さまポカポカ、こころもポカポカ♥
フルーツバスケット
メガヒット!
十二支ホームコメディ
第57回
どこか懐かしい5月の風…
まるでお母さんのにおいの様に…。
高屋奈月

▶ *Fruits Basket* Chapter 57 color opening spread

創刊28周年記念号!!
高屋奈月
フルーツバスケット

◀ *Hana to Yume* Issue 11, 2002 cover

花とゆめCOMICS
フルーツバスケット
高屋奈月 10

Hana to Yume Comics
Volume 10
Published October 2002

十二支ホームコメディ
フルーツバスケット
第60回
高屋奈月

▲ *Fruits Basket* Chapter 60 color opening page

草摩の頂点にたつ存在…!!
十二支コメディ 第62回
フルーツバスケット
高屋奈月

▲ *Fruits Basket* Chapter 62 color opening page

2002

Issue 15

Chapter 60
Color opening page +
30 pages
P: Summer-colored fragrance (mini cushion)

Issue 16

Chapter 61
30 pages

Issue 17

Chapter 62
Color opening page +
30 pages

All (Issues 15–17): Little character ★ fastener accessory

Issue 18

Front: Silver peel game (Find your dance partner!)
Bonus: Mini-cute! towel

All: All-Star ★ trading card set

Issue 19

Cover
Chapter 63
Color opening page +
30 pages

Issue 20

Chapter 64
30 pages

Issue 21

Chapter 65
Color opening spread +
30 pages

All (Issues 19–21): All-Star ★ trading card set

Issue 22

P: Rice ball lunchbox
Bonus: Stand-up ♥ postcard

Issue 23

Dining table: 2 pages

HANAYUME
19
日高万里
ひつじの涙
高屋奈月
フルーツバスケット
オールスター★
トレーディング
カード

▲ *Hana to Yume* Issue 19, 2002 cover

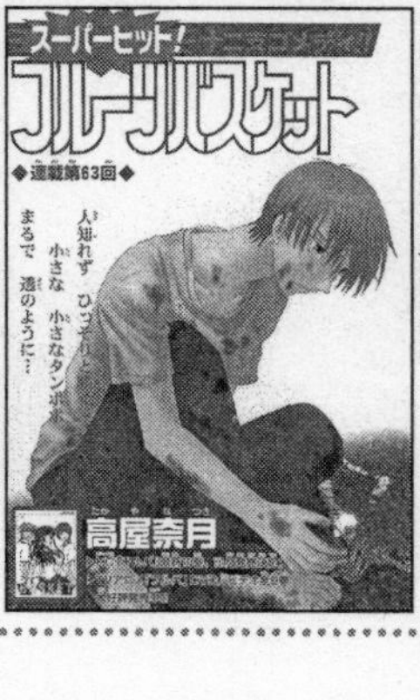
スーパーヒット!
フルーツバスケット
連載第63回
高屋奈月

▲ *Fruits Basket* Chapter 63 color opening page

出会いがいっぱい♥ オシャレして街へ出よう!
十二支コメディ 第65回
フルーツバスケット
高屋奈月

▲ *Fruits Basket* Chapter 65 color opening spread

花とゆめCOMICS
フルーツバスケット
高屋奈月 11

Hana to Yume Comics
Volume 11
Published February 2003

MOGE!
MORNING!

守りたいです…皆さんが歩んでいく道を———できる限りの力で!!
新章スタート!!!
フルーツバスケット
高屋奈月

▲ *Fruits Basket* Chapter 66 color spread

24
ハッピー&メリーXmas号♥
フルーツバスケット
高屋奈月

▲ *Hana to Yume* Issue 24, 2002 cover

2002 — Issue 24
Cover
Chapter 66
Color spread + 30 pages

2003 — Issue 1
Chapter 67
30 pages

P: *Hana-Yume* All-Star ★ autographed New Year's card
Bonus: 2003 All-Star calendar

Issue 2
Chapter 68
30 pages

Bonus: Schedule book

Issue 3
Dining table: 1 page
P: *Hana-Yume* dream ★ item (zodiac clock)
Bonus: Triple CD bag

Issue 4
Chapter 69
Color opening spread + 30 pages

Issue 5
Chapter 70
30 pages

Issue 6
Cover
Chapter 71
Color opening page + 30 pages

Issue 7
Bonus: Spring school notebook

All: Happy character ♥ strap

フルーツバスケット
高屋奈月

▲ *Fruits Basket* Chapter 71 color opening page

6
2003
フルーツバスケット
高屋奈月
しゃにむにGO
羅川真里茂
ハッピーキャラ♥ストラップ

▲ *Hana to Yume* Issue 6, 2003 cover

フルーツバスケット
十二支コメディ連載 第69回
高屋奈月

▲ *Fruits Basket* Chapter 69 color opening spread

花とゆめCOMICS
フルーツバスケット
高屋奈月
12

Hana to Yume Comics
Volume 12
Published June 2003

WHAT A LOVELY MORNING...

メガヒット連載再開！
十二支ホームコメディ
第72回
もう うつむいて
生きたくないから…
フルーツバスケット
高屋奈月
▲ *Fruits Basket* Chapter 72

2003

Issue 8
Chapter 72
Color opening page +
30 pages

Issue 9
Chapter 73
30 pages

Issue 10
Chapter 74
30 pages

All: Yuki & Kyo exciting ♥ room items

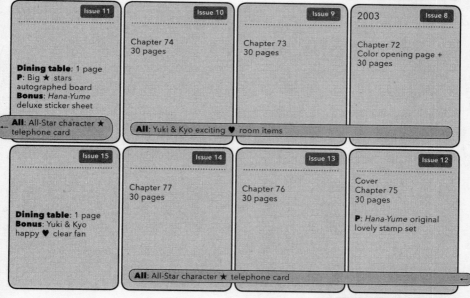

Issue 11
Dining table: 1 page
P: Big ★ stars
autographed board
Bonus: *Hana-Yume*
deluxe sticker sheet

← **All**: All-Star character ★
telephone card

Issue 12
Cover
Chapter 75
30 pages

P: *Hana-Yume* original
lovely stamp set

Issue 13
Chapter 76
30 pages

Issue 14
Chapter 77
30 pages

All: All-Star character ★ telephone card ←

Issue 15
Dining table: 1 page
Bonus: Yuki & Kyo
happy ♥ clear fan

高屋奈月
フルーツバスケット
2003 ALL STAR
▲ *Hana to Yume* Issue 12, 2003 cover

花とゆめCOMICS
フルーツバスケット
高屋奈月 13

Hana to Yume Comics
Volume 13
Published November 2003

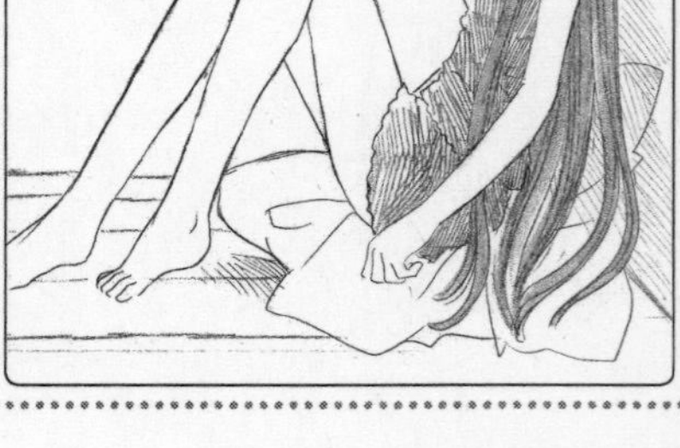
NOT GOOD AT SLEEPING

18
ドキ・ワク・が待ってる♥新学期!!
日高万里
ひつじの涙

▶ Hana to Yume Issue 18, 2003 cover

十二支ホームコメディ第78回
超人気
フルーツバスケット
高屋奈月

▶ Fruits Basket Chapter 78 color opening spread

2003

Issue 16

Chapter 78
Color opening spread +
30 pages

Issue 17

Chapter 79
30 pages

P: Super-big towel

Issue 18

Cover
Chapter 80
30 pages

Issue 19

Dining table: 1 page
P: Flower can
(Tohru lamé mirror /
manicure set)
Bonus: Notepad &
desk pad

All: Love ♥ can badge collection

Issue 20

Chapter 81
Color opening spread +
30 pages
P: Dream can
(Yuki passcase /
Kyo cell phone holder /
lamé pen set /
boys' postcard)

Issue 21

Chapter 82
30 pages

Issue 22

Chapter 83
30 pages

Issue 23

Dining table: 1 page
P: Deluxe poster
calendar

オレってクール☆
すすめ!学園防衛隊!!
みんなのリーダー!!
十二支コメディ第81回
フルーツバスケット
高屋奈月

▶ Fruits Basket Chapter 81 color opening spread

花とゆめCOMICS
フルーツバスケット
高屋奈月 14

Hana to Yume Comics
Volume 14
Published April 2004

DEEP
SLEEP

HANAYUME
HELLO
30th
しゃにむにGO
BIGプロジェクト

▶ *Hana to Yume* Issue 1, 2004 cover

2003 — Issue 24
Chapter 84
30 pages

2004 — Issue 1
Cover
Chapter 85
30 pages
P: All-Star autographed New Year's card
Bonus: All-Star ★ 2004 calendar

Issue 2
Chapter 86
30 pages
Front: *Hana-Yume* trivia

Issue 3
Dining table: 1 page
P: Kyo's cat rucksack
Bonus: Cutie ♥ mechanical pencil

All (Issues 24–3): Zodiac figure

Issue 4
Chapter 87
Color opening spread + 30 pages

Issue 5
Chapter 88
30 pages
P: Twin-Star ★ card

Issue 6
Chapter 89
30 pages
P: Happy White Day (POM cushion)

Issue 7
Front: Zodiac lunch box recipe
P: Cherry-blossom-viewing goods (luncheon mat)

Issue 8
Bonus: Go! Go! School clear file folder

All (Issues 5–8): Super ♥ beautiful clear poster

優しい1年になりますように…
メガヒット！十二支ホームコメディ 第87回
フルーツバスケット
高屋奈月
十二支の宴――今年の主役は
申年のりっちゃん！
彼のように 優しく穏やかな
年になるといいわ♥

▶ *Fruits Basket* Chapter 87 color opening spread

花とゆめCOMICS
フルーツバスケット
高屋奈月
15

Hana to Yume Comics
Volume 15
Published September 2004

フルーツバスケット
高屋奈月
日高万里
V・B・ローズ
創刊30周年メモリアル特大号!!

▶ Hana to Yume Issue 11, 2004 cover

透の母＝今日子、父＝勝也の出会いが今…!!
フルーツバスケット
高屋奈月
NEWS

▶ Fruits Basket Chapter 90 color opening spread

2004

Issue 9

Chapter 90
Color opening spread +
30 pages

Issue 10

Chapter 91
30 pages

Issue 11

Cover
Chapter 92
30 pages

P: *Hana-Yume* All-Star ★ image fragrance & autographed card / super dream (notebook computer with wallpaper, etc.)

Issue 12

Bonus: Fortune ★ oil-blotting paper

Issue 13

Chapter 93
30 pages

Issue 14

Chapter 94
30 pages

P: Flower-T (Kyo T-shirt)

Issue 15

Chapter 95
30 pages

Issue 16

Dining table: 1 page

花とゆめCOMICS
フルーツバスケット
高屋奈月
16

Hana to Yume Comics
Volume 16
Published January 2005

19
9/20
V・B・ローズ
日高万里
フルーツバスケット
高屋奈月
スキップ・ビート!
仲村佳樹

▶ *Hana to Yume* Issue 19, 2004 cover

NEWS
連載100回記念★
第2回キャラコン
開催決定!!
それぞれの心模様を…
CHECK! チェック!!
高屋奈月
フルーツバスケット

▶ *Fruits Basket* Chapter 96 color opening spread

2004

Issue 17
Chapter 96
Color opening spread + 30 pages
Front: Character-contest solicitation
P: Original business card

Issue 18
Chapter 97
30 pages

Issue 19
Cover
Chapter 98
30 pages

P: Cute! ♥ Practical! ★ stamp set
Bonus: Cutie ♥ cell phone sticker

Issue 20
Dining table: 1 page

All: Über-popular ♥ second book card

Issue 21
Chapter 99
30 pages

Dining table: 1 page
Front, **P**: At your fingertips! Exciting ★ makeup character nail course (nail chips)

Issue 22
Chapter 100
Color opening spread + 30 pages
Front: Character-contest results

Issue 23
Chapter 101
30 pages

Issue 24
Dining table: 1 page
P: Communication tool (Me-mail shot + telephone card) / Christmas ★ item (jewelry box)

祝!
連載第100回
&夾V2達成!!
たっくさんのご声援ありがとう――!!!
第1位
草摩 夾
第2位
本田 透
第3位
草摩由希
フルーツバスケット
高屋奈月
MATSUKI TAKAYA

▶ *Fruits Basket* Chapter 100 color opening spread

花とゆめCOMICS
フルーツバスケット
高屋奈月
17

Hana to Yume Comics
Volume 17
Published May 2005

SHE'S NOT WAKING UP
ZZZZ...

▲ *Hana to Yume* Issue 3, 2005 cover

あんた達！
仕事は!?
2005年
フルーツバスケット
高屋奈月

▲ *Fruits Basket* Chapter 103 color opening spread

2005 — Issue 1

Chapter 102
30 pages

P: 2005 All-Star ★ autographed New Year's card
Bonus: 2005 All-Star calendar

Issue 2

Chapter 103
Color opening spread + 30 pages

Issue 3

Cover
Chapter 104
30 pages

P: *Hana-Yume* total original picture reproduction set
Bonus: Tohru's mood ♥ roly-poly stamp

Issue 4

Dining table: 2 pages
Front: *Hana-Yume* competency test
Bonus: *Sparkling Wonderful ★ CD*

Issue 5

Chapter 105
Color opening page + 30 pages

Issue 6

Chapter 106
30 pages

Issue 7

Chapter 107
30 pages

Bonus: *Hana-Yume* All-Star stickers

Issue 8

Dining table: 1 page
Bonus: Yun-yun little ♥ memo & Kyon little ♥ file folder

Issue 9

Dining table: 1 page
P: *Hana-Yume* mega-hits book card

せめて ひととき 安らかな眠りを…
メガヒット！十二支ホームコメディ 第105話
フルーツバスケット
高屋奈月
MATSUKI TAKAYA

▲ *Fruits Basket* Chapter 105 color opening page

花とゆめCOMICS
フルーツバスケット
高屋奈月 18

Hana to Yume Comics
Volume 18
Published September 2005

AWAKE SUPER-EARLY
GOOD MORNING, KUNIMITSU.
YOU BEAT ME AGAIN!! DID YOU EVER ACTUALLY GO TO BED!?

メガヒット★十二支コメディ
フルーツバスケット
第110回
利津から紅野へ
"絆"に縛られた者たちの苦しみを
翼を失うことで真の翼を得た鳥は
どんな想いで見つめるのだろう…
高屋奈月

▲ *Fruits Basket* Chapter 110 color opening spread

フルーツバスケット
高屋奈月

▲ *Hana to Yume* Issue 11, 2005 cover

2005

Issue 10
Chapter 108
30 pages

Issue 11
Cover
Chapter 109
30 pages

Issue 12
Chapter 110
Color opening spread + 30 pages
P: *Furuba*-style iPod mini

Issue 13
Dining table: 1 page
Bonus: *Furuba* boys' silver peel book (book card with present)

Issue 14
Chapter 111
30 pages

P: Special *Furuba* cold container

Issue 15
Chapter 112
30 pages

Issue 16
Chapter 113
30 pages

Issue 17

花とゆめCOMICS
フルーツバスケット
高屋奈月 19

Hana to Yume Comics
Volume 19
Published January 2006

MORRRNING...

透の…慊人の想いが止められない…!!
フルーツバスケット
高屋奈月

▶ Fruits Basket Chapter 115 color opening spread

花とゆめ
18
フルーツバスケット
高屋奈月

▶ Hana to Yume Issue 18, 2005 cover

2005

Issue 18

Cover
Chapter 114
30 pages

Issue 19

Chapter 115
Color opening spread +
30 pages
Bonus: Colorful ♥
3-color pen set

All: PINKY:st.Tohru ♥ dress-up set

Issue 20

Chapter 116
30 pages

Issue 21

Bonus: Romantic
zodiac horoscope ♥
desk pad

Issue 22

Chapter 117
30 pages

Issue 23

Chapter 118
30 pages

Issue 24

Chapter 119
30 pages

2006

Issue 1

Dining table: 1 page
P: All-Star autographed
New Year's card / *Hana-Yume* ★ All-Star quiz &
present (tote bag set)
Bonus: 2006 All ★ Star
calendar

花とゆめCOMICS
フルーツバスケット
高屋奈月
20

Hana to Yume Comics
Volume 20
Published May 2006

MMM...

フルーツバスケット
高屋奈月
▶ Hana to Yume Issue 4, 2006 cover

一番近く 一番遠き存在
互いに
相入れぬ「酉」と「戌」……
フルーツバスケット
高屋奈月
HATSUKI TAKAYA
▶ Fruits Basket Chapter 121 color opening spread

2006

Issue 2

Chapter 120
30 pages

Issue 3

Chapter 121
Color opening spread + 30 pages
Front: Shigure's 2006 better fortune dog horoscope
Bonus: Lucky cell phone cleaner with fortune

Issue 4

Cover
Chapter 122
30 pages

P: *Hana-Yume* All-Star ★ iPod nano

Issue 5

Issue 6

Dining table: 1 page
P: Music box

Issue 7

Chapter 123
Color opening page + 30 pages
P: Cat & Rat ★ hand puppets

Issue 8

Chapter 124
30 pages

Issue 9

Chapter 125
30 pages

Front: *Hana-Yume* Japanese power ★ puzzle

Issue 10

Dining table: 1 page
P: All-Star ★ Super original picture reproduction

永遠の「強敵」…!!!
お待たせ★再開!!!
メガヒット★十二支コメディ
フルーツバスケット
高屋奈月
▶ Fruits Basket Chapter 123 color opening page

花とゆめCOMICS
フルーツバスケット
高屋奈月
21

Hana to Yume Comics
Volume 21
Published September 2006

OW!!
MAYBE EVEN REN-SAN SNAGS HER HAIR WITH HER ELBOW WHEN SHE'S TRYING TO GET UP
BISHI (TUG)

ついに 二人が再会――!?
身も心も 溶けあい ひとつになる この瞬間を ずっと 夢みていた――
メガヒット十二支ドラマ
フルーツバスケット
第128回
高屋奈月
NATSUKI TAKAYA
HC最新刊「フルバ」第20巻、絶好調発売中!!

▲ *Fruits Basket* Chapter 128 color opening spread

11
創刊32周年記念号
800
フルーツバスケット
レジャーシート
高屋奈月

▲ *Hana to Yume* Issue 11, 2006 cover

2006

Issue 11

Cover
Chapter 126
30 pages

P: Original ★ Nintendo DS Lite
Bonus: Exciting big leisure sheet

Issue 12

Chapter 127
30 pages

Issue 13

Chapter 128
Color opening spread + 30 pages
Front: Origami memo-pad course
P: Kyo & Yuki cutie face pouch

Issue 14

Dining table: 1 page
P: *Hana-Yume* summer ★ cell phone lottery (Quo card)
Bonus: Zodiac little ★ clip

Issue 15

Chapter 129
30 pages

Issue 16

Chapter 130
Color opening page + 30 pages

Issue 17

Chapter 131
30 pages

Issue 18

Dining table: 1 page
P: Original gram rice crackers
Bonus: Tohru & Kyo couples' ♥ mechanical pencil

伝えたいことがあるんだ
言葉だけじゃなく
触れ合ったこの指先から――
十二支ホームコメディ第130回
フルーツバスケット
高屋奈月

▲ *Fruits Basket* Chapter 130 color opening page

花とゆめCOMICS
フルーツバスケット
高屋奈月
22

Hana to Yume Comics
Volume 22
Published January 2007

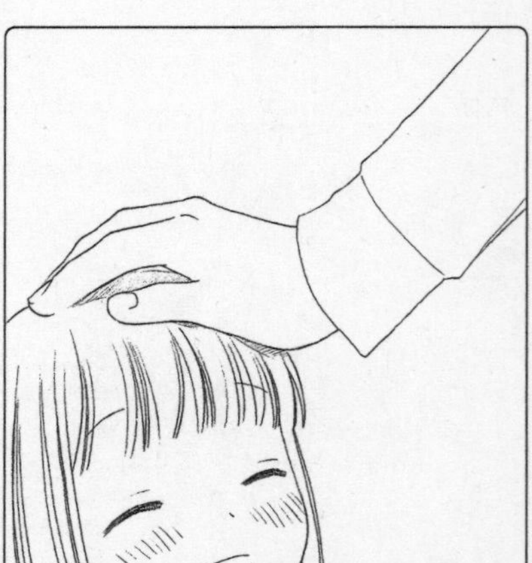

フルーツバスケット
高屋奈月
スキップ・ビート!

▲ *Hana to Yume* Issue 19, 2006 cover

2006 — Issue 19
Cover
Chapter 132
30 pages

P: Original trolley bag

Issue 20
Chapter 133
30 pages

Issue 21
Chapter 134
30 pages

Issue 22
Dining table: 1 page
Bonus: Double-couple clear file folder

Issue 23
Chapter 135
30 pages

Issue 24
Cover
The Final Chapter
Color opening spread + 50 pages
3-page interview
Front: Super-big! *Hana-Yume* ★ cell phone lot (memorial special book card set) / memorial ring necklace / *Xmas Fight* (album)
Bonus: Famous lines karuta

▼ *Fruits Basket*: The Final Chapter color opening spread

最終回
フルーツバスケット
高屋奈月
NATSUKI TAKAYA

フルバ!!FINAL!!
最終回!
フルーツバスケット

▲ *Hana to Yume* Issue 24, 2006 cover

花とゆめCOMICS
フルーツバスケット
高屋奈月
23

Hana to Yume Comics
Volume 23 (Final volume)
Published March 2007

GALLERY
FROM THE VAULT

Bonus

FURUBA IS FINALLY COMPLETE. THANK YOU SO MUCH TO EVERYONE WHO HAS SUPPORTED ME!
THANK YOU FOR BUYING VOLUME 23!
高屋奈月
NATSUKI TAKAYA

[MEMORIAL FILE] STAFF

• Editorial Cooperation •
(pp. 234–293)

Megumi Oouchi, Suzuyo Umezawa
(Studio Amu)

• Design •
(pp. 234–341)

Hanae Kamiya, Yukie Ijiri

TRANSLATION NOTES

COMMON HONORIFICS

no honorific: Indicates familiarity or closeness; if used without permission or reason, addressing someone in this manner would constitute an insult.

-san: The Japanese equivalent of Mr./Mrs./Miss. If a situation calls for politeness, this is the fail-safe honorific.

-sama: Conveys great respect; may also indicate that the social status of the speaker is lower than that of the addressee.

-kun: Used most often when referring to boys, this indicates affection or familiarity. Occasionally used by older men among their peers, but it may also be used by anyone referring to a person of lower standing.

-chan: An affectionate honorific indicating familiarity used mostly in reference to girls; also used in reference to cute persons or animals of either gender.

-senpai: A suffix used to address upperclassmen or more experienced coworkers.

-kouhai: A suffix used to address underclassmen or less experienced coworkers.

-sensei: A respectful term for teachers, artists, or high-level professionals.

Page 42

Red rice: A combination of red beans and sticky rice that is served on auspicious occasions, such as holidays or weddings, which is why their classmates are calling for some now that Tohru and Kyo are officially dating at last. It's a common dish for celebrations because the color red in Japan symbolizes health, happiness, and vitality.

Page 82

"What are you gonna do about a cosigner?": The age of adulthood in Japan is twenty, so Yuki, as a recent high school graduate, is still considered a minor and needs an adult to cosign his lease.

Page 84

"No one can live here, let alone construct a palace!!": The spot Ayame and Mine have found for Yuki's new home is likely Kiyomizu-dera, a Buddhist temple and popular tourist attraction in eastern Kyoto. The expression "to jump off the veranda of Kiyomizu-dera" is similar to the English phrase "to take the plunge," which is fitting for Yuki as he starts a new chapter in his life.

Page 85

"Aren't we just stupidly in love?" / "Yep, you're certainly stupid.": In Japanese, Kakeru is saying he and Komaki are a *bakappuru*, a popular amalgamation of *baka* ("foolish") and *kappuru* ("couple").

Page 92
Otou-sama: A very respectful term for a father (or father figure, as in this case).

Page 155
***Tororo* soba**: Cold soba noodles with grated yam, a reference to their first lunch together back in Volume 5.

Page 184
Hana to Yume: *Fruits Basket* originally ran in the Japanese manga magazine *Hana to Yume* ("Flowers and Dreams"). *Hana-Yume* is a twice-monthly girls' magazine that often includes cute extras for subscribers (see the *Fruits Basket* Serialization History section of this book for examples of the *Furuba*-themed prizes!). Almost all of Takaya-sensei's works have been published in this magazine.

Page 190
"*Nageshi soumen!*": He means *nagashi soumen*. *Soumen* are thin white noodles, and *nagashi* means "flowing." Eating *nagashi soumen* is an experience: Chilled noodles flow down a bamboo "water slide" and are plucked out along the way by diners on either side with chopsticks.

Page 192
Dodoitsu: *Dodoitsu* is a form of poetry unique to Japan. Unlike haiku, which are typically serious and often center around nature, *dodoitsu* are usually comical and deal in everyday subjects, such as work life or romantic struggles. It's one of the longer forms of Japanese poetry, consisting of four unrhyming lines of 7-7-7-5 syllables.

Page 194
"They're sure to thrill you to the bone[...]!" / "You mean grill you to the bone...": They both mean "chill you to the bone." Late summer in Japan is the season for all things scary—the idea being that scary stories (and haunted houses) send chills down your spine, making them a great way to "cool off" from the summer heat.

Page 203
The Hana to Yume: A bimonthly magazine that mainly publishes extra side stories and bonus episodes for the various series published in the main *Hana to Yume* magazine.

Page 205
Dried sardines: Machi is offering Nao dried sardines because they are high in calcium. In Japan, there's a folk belief that calcium deficiency causes grumpiness.

Page 207

Year-end gift: Gift giving has two official seasons in Japan, June/July (midyear) and December (year-end). The idea is to express gratitude and hope for continued favor among coworkers, clients, and relatives (technically friends as well, but this is not as common). Edible gifts of fruit, meat, rice crackers, and sweets are most common, as well as sake.

Page 211

Momotaro: One of Japan's most famous folk tales. An elderly couple finds a giant peach floating down a stream. When they open the peach, they find a little boy inside and name him Momotaro (lit. "Peach Boy"). Years later, Momotaro leaves the village, gathering talking animal comrades (a dog, a monkey, and a pheasant) as he goes off to fight a band of ogres on a distant island. When he returns victorious, he goes back to living with his parents, happily ever after.

Page 241

Momijizuki: The ninth month of the lunar calendar and the month Momiji is named after. Literally, "month of fallen leaves."

Page 243

Ayamezuki: The fifth month of the lunar calendar and the month Ayame is named after. Literally, "month of irises."

Page 246

Isuzukuretsuki: The sixth month of the lunar calendar and the month Isuzu is named after. Literally, "month of cool evenings."

Page 248

Odakaritsuzuki: The ninth month of the lunar calendar and the month Ritsu is named after. Literally, "cutting-the-rice month."

Page 249

Kurenoharu: The third month of the lunar calendar and the month Kureno is named after. Literally, "the end of spring."

Page 250

Shigurezuki: The tenth month of the lunar calendar and the month Shigure is named after. Literally, "month of showers in late autumn."

Page 251

Kagurazuki: The eleventh month of the lunar calendar and the month Kagura is named after. Literally, "month of ancient Shinto music and dancing."

Page 274
White Day: The mirror-image holiday of Valentine's Day. On March 14, males are supposed to give "return gifts" to girls and women who gave them chocolate on Valentine's Day. Candy and cookies are the norm.

Page 276
Golden Week: Golden Week is the popular spring holiday in Japan, typically running from the end of April to the beginning of May. Many workers can take off during this period, which is actually four national holidays rounded off to a week: Shouwa Day (April 29), which honors the birthday of the Shouwa emperor, Hirohito, who reigned from 1926–1989; Constitution Memorial Day (May 3), which celebrates the founding of the Constitution of Japan in 1947; Greenery Day (May 4) for the appreciation of plants; and Children's Day (May 5), in celebration of children.

Page 286
Telephone card: Before the advent of cell phones, telephone cards were a popular form of currency to use with the once-ubiquitous pay phones in Japan. These were often used as promotional items and could be collected as well.

Page 332
Karuta: *Karuta* is a type of card-matching game. A reader will call out the beginning of a phrase or poem, and players will try to find the matching card. Since this was a "*Furuba* famous lines" *karuta*, it most likely had memorable lines from the series.

Fruits Basket

COLLECTOR'S EDITION

Fruits Basket

COLLECTOR'S EDITION

Fruits Basket

NATSUKI TAKAYA

Translation: Sheldon Drzka • Lettering: Lys Blakeslee

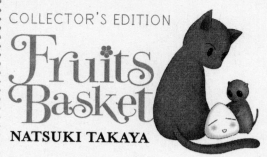

Fruits Basket Collector's Edition, Vol. 12 by Natsuki Takaya

First published in Japan in 2016 by HAKUSENSHA, INC., Tokyo.
English language translation rights in U.S.A., Canada and U.K. arranged with HAKUSENSHA, INC., Tokyo through Tuttle-Mori Agency, Inc., Tokyo.

Yen Press
1290 Avenue of the Americas
New York, NY 10104

Visit us at yenpress.com
facebook.com/yenpress
twitter.com/yenpress
yenpress.tumblr.com
instagram.com/yenpress

First Yen Press Edition: April 2017

Yen Press is an imprint of Yen Press, LLC.
The Yen Press name and logo are trademarks of Yen Press, LLC.

Library of Congress Control Number: 2016932692

ISBN: 978-0-316-50176-7

10 9 8 7 6 5 4 3 2 1

BVG

Printed in the United States of America

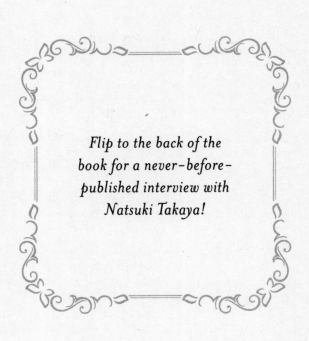

Flip to the back of the book for a never-before-published interview with Natsuki Takaya!

COLLECTOR'S EDITION

Fruits Basket

started from scratch. Please imagine they were "renovated."

Interviewer: Ah-ha-ha! (LOL) You originally planned for *Another* to run for three volumes, but I think many of your readers are hoping you expand the story and continue it.

Takaya: I'm basically trying to make it so you can read it without knowing anything about the *Furuba* main story, but for those who have read it, there's a feeling of "Wow, you've gotten so big! How are you parents doing?" (LOL) I hope you can get the sense that they're relatives. The ages of the kids are a little too close, but it's manga, so I made the choice to go with the fun option over something more realistic. I don't plan for the parents to appear, but I'll be pleased if readers are able to pick up signs from the kids that they live in happy households......I will say right here that I can't have all the next-generation children appear. I definitely couldn't fit the story into three volumes if I did that......

Interviewer: From here on out, will the major focus be on Sawa's growth and the changes she goes through?

Takaya: I would say so. Sawa is a new character who started in *Another* and knows nothing about the Sohma family, so I hope readers calmly watch over her as she gets mixed up with the Sohma family and changes in her own Sawa-centric way!

NATSUKI TAKAYA LONG INTERVIEW
From Comic Natalie's Natsuki Takaya interview (December 2015)

WHERE'S TOHRU-KUN AND KYO-KUN?
HEY, KNOCK THAT OFF!
YOU SHOULD CALL THEM GRANDMA AND GRANDPA!
BUT TOHRU-KUN TOLD ME I COULD CALL HER BY HER NAME!
IF YOU'RE LOOKING FOR GRANDMA AND GRANDPA...
...THEY WENT FOR A WALK.
AWW...
THEY LEFT ME BEHIND AGAIN!
DON'T INTERRUPT THEIR PRIVATE LOVEY-DOVEY TIME, HONEY.
LOVEY-DOVEY, LOVEY-DOVEY! THEY'RE SO LUCKY!
THEY'RE ALWAYS LIKE THAT!
LET'S WALK TOGETHER...

I Hope You Can Get the Sense That They're Relatives

Interviewer: Now I'd like to ask you about the next generation after Tohru and friends, as featured in *Fruits Basket Another*. At the end of the final chapter of *Furuba*, Tohru's child and grandchild make a brief appearance. At that time, were you thinking about their characters and personalities to some extent?

Takaya: In broad strokes. But actually, until I first put them down on storyboards, new characters have a hazy kind of existence in my head. Making exact decisions about them didn't happen until I wrote and drew them in the storyboard stage for Chapter 1 of *Another*. I decided I wouldn't have the set-up be anything that would deny what was achieved in *Furuba*'s main story. I didn't want to do that. I wanted to create a feeling of happiness radiating from the children.

Interviewer: We know Sawa is extremely afraid of becoming a burden on others and that she enters Kaibara High School, where she becomes involved with Mutsuki, a boy with the surname of Sohma. That's the basic synopsis, but what can you tell me about the story?

Takaya: I started by deciding on Mutsuki. I made other vague decisions, but during the process of getting it down on paper, many things changed quite a bit, especially Sawa. Actually, I had ideas for things that happened after the main story for both *Phantom Dream* and *Tsubasa: Those with Wings* too, but in the end I didn't have the chance to draw them, so getting to do this makes me happy on a personal level. Incidentally, with *Phantom Dream*, the story would've been about the grandchild's child and Hira, while Hil would've been the main character in a *Tsubasa* follow-up. That brings back memories... What am I going on about? (LOL)

高屋奈月
翼を持つ者
1
Tsubasa: Those with Wings

高屋奈月
幻影夢想
1
Phantom Dream

Interviewer: I think your longtime fans would love that! It's been a while for you, so how was it drawing Kaibara High School and the school uniforms in *Another*?

Takaya: I've drawn high school uniforms here and there over the years, so I didn't feel anything special while drawing them. But I totally forgot how to draw the school and the Sohma mansion, so I

volumes—I might have even been pretty nervous about it. But that's not unique to *Furuba*. I always go over my projected number......I've already underestimated with *Furuba Another*—at first, the plan was to finish that series in three volumes.

Twinkle Stars, available from Yen Press!

Interviewer: I'm looking forward to the volumes of *Another* too! In the *Banquet* fan book, you said that while *Furuba* was being serialized, you always felt burdened with "responsibility." What kind of responsibility was that?

Takaya: That was the responsibility to bring *Furuba* to a decent conclusion. After I finished the series, I was a wreck in mind and body. To be honest, I was thinking about giving up being a manga artist, but I just couldn't make a clean break. Still, I know I'll never create a series that surpasses *Furuba*, and I never intended to try, so I thought, "Okay, from now on, I'll create a series that reflects my own tastes and at my own pace." And that turned out to be my next series, *Twinkle Stars*. I love that series for being most unabashedly me, free of extra trappings.

Interviewer: *Twinkle Stars* and *Furuba* are both series that stick in the mind as being about people connecting with one another, but *Twinkle* lacks the fantasy element and seems to be more down-to-earth.

Takaya: It's very plain, but that's what I like about it. If you start reading with a carefree attitude, you might take an emotional beating, so be forewarned. (LOL) But to get back to what I was saying, as I wrote in one of the *Furuba* fan books, I've always wanted to create a "next generation" sequel somewhere. When the release of these collector's editions was decided on, I thought, "Right here and now is the only timing I'll have to do it!" I wasn't in great physical condition though, so working on that and *Liselotte & Witch's Forest* simultaneously was just impossible, so I put *Lise* on hiatus. But once I'm done with *Another*, I intend to return to *Lise*. And when I do, I think it'll be serialized online too.

Liselotte & Witch's Forest
1
NATSUKI TAKAYA

Liselotte & Witch's Forest, available from Yen Press!

I Was Shaken When I Couldn't Let Shigure Get Punched

Interviewer: Earlier you said you had the ending in mind from the very beginning. Did the flow of the entire story go as you planned it, or were there any moments that differed from your initial plans?

WHATEVER RESULTS ARE IN STORE...
...BE SURE YOU'RE READY FOR THEM.
I DON'T KNOW IF IT WILL BE YUKI OR KYO... OR MAYBE EVEN HONDA-KUN.
BUT SOMEONE IS GOING TO SOCK YOU IN THE JAW ONE OF THESE DAYS.
AH-HA-HA— YOU'RE PROBABLY RIGHT—
I CAN'T STAND PAIN, BUT THERE'S NOTHING I CAN DO ABOUT IT—
I DON'T LIKE YOUR SHOTS EITHER—
THEY HURT LIKE HELL!
I'M NOT GOING TO BE YOUR ALLY.

Takaya: There were major and minor changes, but one that stands out the most is Shigure not getting punched.

Interviewer: Not getting punched......by which character?

Takaya: In Chapter 16, there's a scene where Hatori tells Shigure, "I don't know if it will be Yuki or Kyo...or maybe even Honda-kun. But someone is going to sock you in the jaw one of these days," but by the time I got to the climax of the story, Yuki and Kyo had both become more emotionally mature than I had originally envisioned, so I couldn't have either of them punch Shigure. If they had, I think the reaction would've been, "What's wrong with them!?" As an author, I was psyched to have Shigure get punched, so I was a little bummed out when I couldn't let it happen.

Interviewer: You were all set to have him get slugged. (LOL)

Takaya: But I was also happy. I was really happy when the characters behaved differently than what I'd originally imagined. That's pretty unusual.

Interviewer: On Twitter you've said that you made a conscious effort to change the art, and toward the end of *Furuba*, it did look like you altered the design to fall in line with the characters' growth. What were you aiming for when you decided to do that?

Takaya: I didn't alter the art because I wanted to. One reason the art changed was as a result of my medical issue, which I'm still sorry about to this day. I apologize for that tweet too, although I've forgotten about it. I probably meant to say I was consciously trying to keep the art from eventually looking "old-fashioned." Maybe that's what I meant. I don't think of myself as a skilled artist, but I do want to strive for my best.

Interviewer: In a sidebar in Volume 21, you mentioned that you went "one volume over" than what you imagined. What events did you expand on more than planned?

Takaya: Actually, it's just that I simply underestimated how many volumes it would take. (LOL) From the beginning, my editor and friends told me, "You won't be able to finish it in that number of volumes!" Why did I try to set and keep the number low? For some reason, I felt as if it wasn't good to increase my estimated number of

FAREWELL.

I Want to Show the Characters Overcoming Darkness

Interviewer: (LOL) Looking back on the story as a whole, are there any moments that especially left an impression on you?

Takaya: I'd have to say the final chapter. That and the scene with Kyoko-san in the penultimate chapter are deeply moving to me. Even though I wrote and drew it myself, I nearly cried......Also the chapter when the curse breaks at last.

Interviewer: Many of the scenes near the end, then.

Takaya: They're especially memorable to me. I think people often get the wrong idea, but I don't particularly like writing and drawing painful, heavy emotions and events. In fact, I would avoid writing them if I could get away with it. I'd like to create nothing but fun things! (LOL) But when I want to show the characters accomplishing something or finding an answer, I can't cut short the tough moments, because all of that is part of the process leading up to it. If I want to show the "light," I have to also show the "darkness." More than anything, I want to show the characters overcoming that. Because that's my goal, I brace myself and shoulder through the tough moments too.

...LET'S STILL FACE OUR FEARS.
THE MOST IMPORTANT THING...
...IS THE DESIRE TO OVERCOME OUR WEAKNESSES.

Interviewer: *Furuba* has a lot of monologues and lines that really resonate. When do these kinds of lines come to you?

Takaya: Thank you! But it wasn't like I, as the creator, was thinking, "I'm gonna give you a cool thing to say!" I was always just trying to express the characters' feelings.

Interviewer: Are there any especially memorable phrases for you?

Takaya: "Desire to overcome weakness" is a phrase I came up with during my high school years...It's what I felt at the time, which was a very hard period for me.

go about getting close to all these characters and showing us their inner selves?

Takaya: This isn't just with *Furuba*, but the way I work on all my series is to set up "stepping-stones" right off the bat. I arrange the important moments and emotions, and then it's as if I "take steps" toward them. The stepping-stones themselves don't move much. But how do I move from stone to stone? That's where I make adjustments all the time. But that part of the job takes place in my head, and I'm bad at explaining it to my editor. I'm also not very good at explaining character personalities, emotions, and intentions...I tell my editor, "It'll all be in the storyboards, so please just wait." (LOL) *Furuba* has a lot of characters, so it was difficult to establish each character's individual point of view. A lot of time has passed since it ended, so I can't clearly remember how it was back then, but I knew if I didn't write enough, the feelings wouldn't get across...but if I wrote too much, the story would become too long...So I was always thinking about how to weave it all together.

I WON'T SEE...
...ARISA AGAIN.

Interviewer: There are many characters, some of which must be easier to draw than others. In a sidebar, you wrote that it was very hard to draw Kureno.

WHO
▲ Chihiro from *Twinkle Stars*

Takaya: Kureno-san kept not listening to me when I'd say, "Okay, this is how I planned this moment will go." It's as if he disagreed with my ideas—and because he disagreed, he wouldn't budge! I would think, "What's with you!?" but I really am fond of Kureno-san. I love those almost self-destructive characters whose kindness causes their own undoing (but no one around them realizes it). Chihiro-kun in *Twinkle Stars* was my next character in that vein. I know these characters tend to be hated, but I can't bring myself to hate them—and in fact, I think creating characters like that is a hallmark of my manga. So yeah......(LOL)

Interviewer: What about the main character, Tohru? You've said, "I want to talk about her most of all—and yet I feel as if I shouldn't talk about her."

Takaya: Not just about Tohru-kun, but the series itself too. Sometimes I really want to talk all night about them! I often feel like that. But you know...I don't want to interfere with what the reader feels. For example, if I go, "It's like this and means this," if there are readers who didn't feel that way when they read the manga, it's as if I'm telling those readers their interpretation is "incorrect." So I wouldn't want to make any public statement about it. However, if you get me at a private gathering, I'll blab on and on about it. Until morning! (LOL)

Takaya: As a rule, I don't go back and read my old works, but I did flip through to check……On the whole, I was impressed by the power of my youth. (LOL) In both a good way and a bad way. I was young then, so I could draw a lot. There are things I could draw then that I can't now and things I can draw now, being older, that I couldn't back then.

Interviewer: *Furuba* was completed in 2006 after a nine-year run. What did that work mean to you? In a sidebar in the final volume, you wrote, "To an author, there is no true 'farewell' to a work, so coming to its conclusion isn't that sad."

THANK YOU...
THANK YOU.
...THANK YOU...
...TOHRU.
THANK YOU.

Takaya: The story itself is completed, but I've still been doing *Furuba*-related work every now and then here and there, so it never left me completely. I guess it feels like *Furuba* is always with me. I forget the details of my more complicated works, and *Phantom Dream* and *Tsubasa: Those with Wings* are in a deep slumber, but I never feel like *Furuba* is gone.

It Came Into Being from the Final Chapter

Interviewer: I see. Now I would like to ask you about when the series was being published. Some of the charm of *Furuba* comes from moments of slapstick and fun arguments among characters. But when you were asked if you'd label it a "domestic comedy" when Volume 1 was published, you wrote, "I don't think of it as a comedy." When you were first working on the series, what was your focal point?

Takaya: *Furuba* is a work that came into being from the scene between Tohru and Yuki in the final chapter. That scene and the monologue from Kyoko-san's last scene are the cornerstones of its foundation. As the story progressed, we did come across more and more comedic situations, and of course I realized that, so I'd often find myself thinking, "Stop it……Stop giving the exact opposite impression of what you're going for……" (LOL)

...HAND IN HAND.
THROUGH THE JOYOUS TIMES...AND THE SAD...
THE CYCLE REPEATING ITSELF, AGAIN AND AGAIN.
THAT'S HOW...

Interviewer: You had quite the dilemma. Tohru is the main character of *Furuba*, but you have many other characters, giving the series an ensemble aspect that allows you to dig deeply into each character's humanity. How did you

NATSUKI TAKAYA LONG INTERVIEW

In 2015, to celebrate the beginning of the *Fruits Basket* collector's edition releases as well as the start of a new series, *Fruits Basket Another*, on *Hana LaLa Online*, the website Comic Natalie conducted a long interview with Natsuki Takaya-sensei. Her thoughts at the time of writing *Furuba* and feelings during the creation of *Another* are shown here.

Furuba Is Always with Me

Interviewer: Congratulations on the release of the *Fruits Basket* collector's editions! When the news hit on Comic Natalie that the first collector's edition would be released and that *Fruits Basket Another* would begin serialization soon, it made a huge impact. We had around forty thousand retweets!

Takaya: Thank you! I would've been happy just having my series republished in mass-market size so people could continue to read it for a long time, but for it to be a special collector's edition, wow......It's amazing. The fans often asked me about putting out a collector's edition, so I'm glad their wishes have been granted.

Interviewer: Even now, people all over the world love this series. Why do you think it won over so many?

Takaya: To this day, I still don't know. (LOL) I want to know that answer myself......! I wonder......But I appreciate it. It makes me really happy.

Interviewer: What kind of thoughts popped into your head as you looked back on the original manuscripts to prepare for the collector's editions? It's been a long time, after all.